# PRAISE FOR *DRYLAND*

"Remarkable. It's realism, but its realism brushes ever so deftly against the allegorical, making the novel shimmer, part diary, part dream."

—**MAGGIE NELSON**, *The Argonauts*

"Sara Jaffe is a damn fine writer and an important new voice."

—**JUSTIN TORRES**, *We the Animals*

"I love it. I don't know that I've ever read a book that felt more sincere, that was so unbesmirched by knowing irony or commentary or authorial interventions. It's a rare and sweet thing."

—**PETER ROCK**, *The Shelter Cycle*

"*Dryland* is a gorgeous, layered, meticulous, clamoring, beating heart of a thing about a sullen teenager swimming and not swimming, kissing and not kissing, in Portland in the days of grunge. It will make you want to swim there and back twenty times without stopping."

—**SARA MARCUS**, *Girls to the Front*

"A coming-of-age story about a young girl's growing awareness—of sexuality, loss, and family truths . . . [W]e relive the awkward agonies of adolescence, so well-sketched by Jaffe. . . Moving sideways with its weight of secrets, this novel never strikes a false note."

—*KIRKUS*

# DRYLAND

## A NOVEL BY

# sara jaffe

Tin House Books

Portland, Oregon & Brooklyn, New York

Published by Tin House Books, Portland, Oregon and Brooklyn, New York

Distributed by W. W. Norton and Company.

Library of Congress Cataloging-in-Publication Data

Jaffe, Sara.

  Dryland / by Sara Jaffe. -- First U.S. edition.

    pages cm

  ISBN 978-1-941040-13-3 (alk. paper)

  I. Title.

  PS3610.A367D79 2015

  811'.6--dc23

2015016031

Lyrics on pages 32 and 170 excerpted from the R.E.M. song "Country Feedback" which appeared on their album *Out of Time*. Lyrics reprinted courtesy of Alfred Publishing.

First US edition 2015
Printed in the USA
Interior design by Diane Chonette
www.tinhouse.com

To my parents, for celebrating me when
I succeeded and letting me feel free to fail

ON THE COVER of Swimmers' World was a swimming guy's face obscured by splashes. On Swimming Monthly a coach in a rose garden. The smell of cigars stuffed the air at Rich's News, and beneath it, a note of stale trading-card gum. On the wall, a sign said No Reading. Rich, if it was Rich, unpacked cigars behind the counter, ignoring me. My monthly or so spot-check of swimming magazines consisted of a practiced skimming: contents, capsules, photos. The cover of Poolside had a blond diver toweling off. If Rich took my skimming as reading and called me out, it would be easy to say I'd been looking for something, and if Rich said, For what? Rich wouldn't.

Next to me, a guy was working. He was pulling magazines off the rack, tearing off their covers, and throwing the magazines and the covers into two piles on the floor. I'd gotten through Swimming Monthly and had just picked up Poolside. The guy said, Poolside, right on. You're a swimmer?

I'd never seen him before. One of the things about coming to Rich's was that nobody who knew me went there. Being at Rich's was like being nowhere. I said, I'm not.

He said, You look like you could be.

I didn't look like anything—my jeans and my raincoat and my flannel and my henley. I said, I'm not.

He said, Right on.

I said, Are you?

He laughed. He touched a bead on a cord around his neck. He had skaterish hair and he was older than me, my brother's age, maybe. He said, Not me. He said, Sorry to interrupt your reading. He smiled like he knew me.

I said, I'm not reading.

He laughed. He said, That sign's just there for the guys who come in to read porn. He made quotes with his fingers when he said read.

The back wall was all magazines in plastic with their titles popping out above blank sheets of paper. A few men stood in front of them. Should someone who didn't know me be talking to me about pornos? Should he be talking like he knew me and making quotes with his fingers? The men at the back wall shouldn't, it seemed, be doing what they were doing in public—scoping pornos behind plastic, hard-ons squirming in their pants.

My finger marked Poolside's centerfold. The guy was still standing right there, as if he had something else to say to me. I turned the pages as fast as I could, barely looking, defeating my purpose. Goggled eyes, ripped abs, smashed boobs flashed by. Swimmers stroked down lanes and water splashed up and hid their faces. The guy ripped off a cover and tossed it in a pile. Any minute he could ask me what I was looking for.

RICH'S WAS ONLY a few blocks up from the River Market. It was raining, surprise. Two rainy days in a row in November meant it wouldn't let up until June. This was the third day. Not that the rain bothered me. Erika showed up and we put up our hoods and walked around the vendors. Neither of us was going to buy anything. Erika wanted to look at the Fimo beads. She looked at a purple and green bead on a brown leather cord and said, I could totally make that. Erika's mom made jewelry that she sometimes sold at the River Market. Erika had used her mom's beading stuff to make me a seed-bead necklace that was as nice as any for sale in the stalls. The prices at the market had gone up or the things we liked now were more expensive—the Guatemala backpacks and the earflap hats. We went because it was what we did, something to do on a Saturday. We got noodles or kettle corn. Erika wanted to go eat our yakisoba by the fountain.

I said, It's raining.

She said, We'll stand under the awning by the coffee shop. She wanted to watch the skater boys doing tricks on their skateboards by the fountain. There were signs that said No Skateboarding but nobody stopped them. Other skaterish boys and girls stood around smoking.

Erika said, Don't you love the smell of cloves?

A couple of the skaters had brown cigarettes. All I could smell was the tobacco from the regular cigarettes. I said, They smell good.

She said, Maybe I should start smoking them. I bet they're not as bad for you as regular cigarettes. She said, But I wouldn't know how to buy them.

I said, You could ask one of those kids, knowing she wouldn't. Or expecting she wouldn't, who knew, she might. She was the one who wanted to stand in the rain and watch these kids skate and smoke cloves. It was generous of me to watch them with her.

The skaters rode their skateboards up on the cement rim of the fountain. Erika said, Do you think that one is cute? I mean, hot?

I said, The one with the pants?

She said, With the purple sweatshirt.

His pants were stupid too, but not as stupid as the other one's. Purple sweatshirt kept flicking his hair out of his eyes while he was trying to jump his skateboard up on the rim. Erika said, Don't you think it's cute how he keeps flicking his hair?

To me flicking hair wasn't something to call cute or not cute. I said, Sure.

Erika said, You don't have to think so just because I think so.

I said, Okay.

She said, Which one do you think is the cutest?

They all looked fine. It really was stupid that skaters had huge pants and hair in front of their faces when they were trying to do something graceful. The guy at Rich's hadn't looked like a skater. He'd looked like what, a college student? A guitar player? I pointed to one with slightly smaller pants and a black-and-green flannel and brown hair back in a baseball cap. He was skating around the fountain in circles, smoothly dodging benches and trash and other skaters.

Erika said, Don't point! She said, He is cute. He looks like a little rascal. You like that type.

Whatever that meant. My guy rolled to a stop and stretched his arms. He took off his baseball cap and his long hair went down past his shoulders. It was long, soft-looking hair for a guy. It wasn't a guy. It was suddenly so obviously not a guy. My face felt hot and I wanted to take off my raincoat and my flannel. I didn't move. The girl went and sat down on the bench and took off her flannel, and in her T-shirt you could definitely tell she had boobs. It was embarrassing how much like a girl she looked. The guy with the stupidest pants came over and sat down next to her, close to her, and then leaned in his head and kissed her. They were frenching, going at it, right there on the bench at the fountain. None of their friends noticed or looked. The guy and the girl were mouthing each other to pieces in the rain. The girl's hand went for the huge crotch of the guy's stupid pants. Erika said, Whoa. If she said anything to me about how that was the person I picked, I'd be ready for her. I'd blame it on the girl. I'd blame it on the stupid skater clothing. I would say, what was it people said, They should get a room. Erika's guy flicked his hair and took a speeding leap up onto the rim of the fountain and sailed off. Now it was really raining.

MY DAD PASSED me a drumstick and my mom took some slices of white meat. My dad asked how the market had been. My mom asked if I'd bought anything. These were ideas of questions, the sort of paper airplanes of questions my parents felt obligated to lob in my direction over dinner. I could catch them, crumple them, lob them back.

I said, It's gotten too expensive. In my parents' minds the River Market still ran along the river and only sold driftwood and soap. All they could do was take my word for it. I said, A lot of that stuff I could make myself.

I pulled the skin off my drumstick with my teeth. My mind kept veering to the skaters frenching on the bench, to their sloppy tongues, her hand swatting at his crotch. To how the skater girl had been a boy until she wasn't. My mind went to the instant I saw her boobs through her shirt and realized. It was like the photo at the back of The Elephant Man that I couldn't stop myself from turning to again and again as if to make sure it was still as horrible, or to make sure that it hadn't gotten more horrible since I'd seen it last. Maybe I was over the River Market. Maybe Erika and I only went there because we went there, or I only went there because Erika asked me to go.

My mom passed me the cranberries and said, What about Erika, did she buy anything? The jellied cranberry sauce from the can held its shape like a cylinder of Play-Doh. I remembered feeding scoops of Play-Doh into the plastic machine, getting a hold on the plastic lever and giving it all my strength until something gave and wormy tubes of gray-green spaghetti pushed out the holes. What did my mom care what Erika bought or didn't buy? I said, I think she bought a bracelet.

Pledge came over and put her head in my lap. I felt her skull through her thin, soft fur. When the guy at Rich's had caught me scoping Poolside and said I looked like a swimmer I should have said So what or I know or Tell me what you mean. When I'd felt the guy's eyes crawling over my shoulders, I should have told him that he had it wrong. My brother was the swimmer in our family.

THE THING ABOUT the photo in the back of The Elephant Man book, which I hadn't checked out of the library in years, was that you needed the photo to complete the story. It wasn't okay to be willing to read about the Elephant Man and not look at him, though for me to look at the photo and think all the same messed-up thoughts people had thought when they looked at him in person, when he was alive, was wrong, too, maybe more wrong. Every time I looked at the photo of the

Elephant Man, or thought about what he looked like
in the photo, I wanted to not feel what I was feeling:
nauseated, as if my head were a balloon, as if his skin,
if I touched it, would feel like papier-mâché. If he offered his hand I would instantly drop it. The skater girl
thing was entirely different: she was choosing to look
the way she did, and the way she looked didn't seem to
be causing her any problems. Anyone who didn't know
her and who saw her with those boys in that skating
getup would have no reason to think she wasn't one of
them. What was getting me was the moment when she
went from being a boy fumbling skate tricks to a girl
making out on a bench. It wasn't a moment but a gap
between moments, a face with no features. My head felt
like a balloon.

I SAT IN the back of the yearbook room cutting out captions for the mock-up. It was a mindless task, and it was
fine with me. I didn't care about Yearbook. I didn't as-
pire to take photos or be editor the way Erika did, and
I was only there because she'd begged me to join with
her. I took a piece of paper from the stack in front of me,
lifted my scissors, and sliced the caption cleanly.

Erika said, Shit. She showed me the jagged cut she'd
just made. She'd sliced the tip off an A again. She said, Can
you fix it? She said, I'm going to tell them they need to
give us something better to do. Don't you think I should?

I said, I don't mind doing captions.

Erika said, Those girls are so full of themselves. They should stick to soccer. She pointed her scissors at the editors, who were standing at Ms. C.'s desk. For Erika there was something particular to hate about Melanie and Alexis, about soccer girls in general, how they smiled and swung their blonde ponytails but bore down vicious on the field. She said they had fangs that came out when they needed them.

Melanie asked for a volunteer to go make copies. Erika volunteered. She always volunteered and did whatever they asked her to do and complained about it later to me. I didn't mind. If she was out of the room I wouldn't have to sit there waiting for her to bring up something about the skater girl—to say wasn't that funny, or weird, and expect me to say something in response. I picked up the sheet of paper, lifted my scissors, and cut close but not too close to the typed letters.

Alexis said, Julie, right? She was over at my table. She said, Want some pretzels? She sat on the edge of the table and offered the bag to me. She was wearing a soccer sweatshirt that was perfectly oversized. It smelled like fabric softener. I didn't know if I was supposed to put down my scissors or keep working. She said, You're really good at that. She was making the rounds, or she had just come over to talk to me. She said, We were wondering who the one was who was cutting them so neatly. I guess it was you.

I said, Thank you.

She said, We should give you something better to do at some point.

I said, I don't mind. Alexis's hair was really more dirty blonde than blonde.

Alexis said, You're modest. She took her hair out of its ponytail and shook it out a bit. Dirty blonde didn't seem right either. She moved her hair from behind her left shoulder to the front of her left shoulder. She said, What would you like to do, take photos?

I put down my scissors. I had a Polaroid I pulled out every once in a while to take shots of nothing special: Erika on my birthday, Pledge wet with a ball in her mouth, Pledge in the sun. Alexis was leaning on my table as if she had all the time in the world, as if she had nothing else to do. She had a million other things to do. I said, I'm not really a photographer.

Alexis said, Too bad. Are you sure? Her fabric softener smelled clean, like a field.

I said, I really don't mind doing captions for now. If Alexis had offered to teach me how to take photos, I would have said yes, because she seemed as if she'd be a good teacher.

Alexis smiled at me. I didn't see any fangs, or nubs of fangs. She said, Okay, let me know if you change your mind. I think you'd make a great photographer.

Erika came back with the copies. She delivered them and sat back down at the table. She picked up a sheet to cut and said, Ugh, I can't believe we're still doing these. She said, Where did you get those? I'm starving.

Erika had taken Photo and she had a real camera. She knew how to use the darkroom. She'd offered before to teach me, and I could ask her now but no part of me wanted to. It wouldn't be fair, since she was the one who wanted to take photos and Alexis had only asked me. I held out some pretzels to Erika. I said, These? I brought them from home.

RICH'S SMELLED LIKE a million cigars. I picked up Swimmers' World and started at the end, skimming backward through the pages—no real reason, maybe as proof that I wasn't reading. Or as if I'd be more likely to find something if I snuck up on it. The photos I flashed past were blue and more blue: pool water, mostly, and the outdoor shots showed only blue skies. Swimmers in locker rooms dripped on blue tile. Near the front of Swimmers' World was a section that paired photos of swimmers in and out of the pool. Here was Nelson Diebel tearing water apart to win the 100 breaststroke, and here he was eating a plate of spaghetti. Here was Anita Nall, her head lifted for a breath, and here she was cuddling puppies on a blue couch. The bells on the door jingled and an old man came in. The guy from the other day wasn't anywhere.

There was one shot in the spread of a guy swimming freestyle. White water foamed around his face and it was impossible to tell the swimmer's height or body type. Something was familiar in the crook of his arm, or

how the top of his thigh lowered into a kick. If I were to
pick up a camera and take a photo, this was the kind of
photo I would take. It showed the swimmer doing what
he was best at and made it look easy. It made me feel as
if I could know the person in the photo.

The swimmer in the corresponding out-of-the-pool
photo was patting a horse on its neck. He didn't look
like anyone. On my way out Rich looked up and said,
Have a good night, sweetheart. It was dark and rainy at
five o'clock. People wore raincoats if they had raincoats,
soaked hoodies if they didn't. I put up the hood of my
raincoat. It was a thing people said and it was true, only
tourists carried umbrellas. Thin nails of rain hit my hood.
Something in me felt off, and I checked my backpack to
make sure the zippers were closed. I touched my wallet in my front pocket. Maybe I was hungry. The pizza
place next door put out a warm, salty smell. Skater kids
with backpacks leaned against the counter and ate slices.
There was a guy in a beanie who went to my school. He
tossed down the crust of one slice and picked up another.
It was as if he could stand there all evening eating pizza
and not need to worry about getting home for dinner, or
about being too full for dinner when he got there.

The guy shook red pepper flakes onto his pizza. His
hair went in his eyes but he didn't flick it out of the way.
His fingers were long and bony, and he was at least as
cute as the guy Erika had liked. If the skater girl showed
up, I wanted her to be dressed exactly as she had been
the other day, so I could see if she still looked like a boy

now that I knew she wasn't one. If she truly looked that much like a boy, then the mistake would be on her. The skater kid took a big bite of pizza and then went wildly for his soda cup, a gesture too outsized for how spicy the pizza could have been, even if it were smothered in red pepper flakes, which I guessed it was but couldn't see for sure. I was still outside.

Men in jean jackets stood outside the bar across the street, smoking cigarettes in the rain. I thought bars, or most bars, allowed smoking inside. In my gray-blue raincoat I was the same color as the rain and the buildings and the sidewalk. The smoking men stared out at the street. Some people's parents might not have let them walk around downtown in the dark by themselves. With my hood up, I felt invisible. Meaning safe. My shoulders were broad, my height tallish. Most clothes fit me in places and hung off me in others. I was built, so what, like a swimmer, but that didn't mean the guy at Rich's had had any right to say, You look like you could be. That he'd said it was still bugging me. It was bugging me mostly because what did that guy know about swimming, or how a swimmer should or could look.

I passed Rich's and couldn't see in through the fogged-up windows. Every place, it felt like, was becoming impossible for me to go. At the bus stop a homeless guy tried to sell me a transfer, and I could have given him the change in my pocket. I pretended not to hear him. The rain came down hard and there was no room in the bus shelter. I felt my jeans getting soaked at the thigh-line. A packed bus, not mine, pulled up and pulled away. Daylight savings had just happened and it felt darker than it should have for how early it was.

MY MOM TOOK some white meat. My dad passed the salad. I said to my dad, Do you still have that old camera? He asked if I meant the Pentax. I said, I don't know, the one with the strap. The camera I remembered had a braided leather strap. It had a lens that twisted out to make it longer, or maybe it was a separate lens that attached. Alexis hadn't said what kind of camera I'd need, but my Polaroid was definitely not real enough. After dinner I followed my dad downstairs to his office and he got down the camera from a shelf in the closet. It had a wide cloth strap that said Pentax. It looked newer than I remembered. My dad asked if I knew how to work it. The camera was cold from sitting in a closet in the basement for who knew how long. It had real heft to it. I raised the camera and pointed it at my dad. I moved the focus ring and watched him get blurry and clear. He made his Donald Duck face. Sometimes I forgot I had parents.

I pressed the metal button to take the photo. Nothing happened. I said, Something's wrong with it. I said, Maybe it's too cold. My dad moved the wand to advance the film and I heard the little teeth catching. He said he didn't know what was on the rest of the roll, that he couldn't remember the last time he'd used it. He said I was free to take the camera if I wanted it. His footsteps moved up the stairs and sounded across the floor above me. I looped the camera strap around my neck. I pointed it at my dad's desk. I took the lid off his rubber-band box and looked in on that. When the office had been my brother's room the walls might have been blue, but he'd let me in so rarely I couldn't remember. I pointed the camera at the coils of the dead space heater. It was freezing down there.

At nine we all watched L.A. Law in the family room. The main case involved my favorite lawyer, who was arguing on behalf of a client whose baby had gotten sick after chewing on a toy painted with toxic paint. The lawyer for the corporation that made the toy said that parents should watch their kids to make sure they didn't put toys in their mouths. My favorite lawyer was taking the corporation to town. I hadn't noticed before, but she had a thing that she did where she moved a swath of her hair—blondish, shiny as a weapon—from behind her shoulder to in front of it. Alexis hadn't said what kind of photos she'd want me to take. If she had some more downtime we could pull old yearbooks off the shelves and she could show me what she thought I'd be good at. Once I learned the basics and got going, I could see myself hitting my stride. Taking photos might become the thing I did—not because I cared about moving up in Yearbook, but because I was a good photographer. The shelves in our house had a few of my brother's trophies and some old family photos, but the walls were mostly blank space—all that was up in the family room was a

poster from a jazz festival, another of the Golden Gate
Bridge at night. I looked at the blank, beige walls and
saw framed images heaving into focus.

The credits rolled. Pledge lifted herself from her dog
pillow and stretched, her collar jangling. In my room I
took off my sneakers and set them in the middle of my
turquoise wall-to-wall carpet. I sat on my bed and aimed
the camera at them. I aimed across the room at my post-
ers. I was the photographer taking a picture of R.E.M.
standing on a bridge over a river in a place I thought of
as Germany. I focused the shot on the drummer's ear. On
Michael Stipe's eyebrow. No one had conversations about
whether he was cute. I took a painted pinecone I'd made
as a kid and put it on my pillow. I looked at it through
the lens from a couple different angles, but some ridge or
another kept ending up in shadow. Maybe Alexis could
show me the right way to use the camera. She could give
me a lesson or two, no big deal. I put the pinecone back
on its shelf. I'd develop the film as soon as I got through
the rest of the roll, and I'd see what else was on there. My
dad hadn't said how old the film was, it could be a year or
five years. For all I knew it could be rotting in its chamber.

IT TOOK ANOTHER week for Melanie to request volunteers
again, and for Erika to leave the room, and then Melanie,
and then all that were left were a few straggling proofers,
and Ms. C. at her desk, and Alexis, and me. The camera

was wrapped in a bandana at the bottom of my bag. I took it out and unwrapped it and set it on the table. I went back to my captions.

Alexis said, Still cutting? You're a trouper. She offered a bag of yogurt-covered raisins. She said, It's been crazy. Now they're saying we need quotes from three different printers. I nodded. She said, And it's like, why can't we just use the printer we've always used?

The camera sat on the table between us. It pointed toward me.

Alexis said, Is that your camera?

I said, I borrowed it.

She said, That looks like a nice one. I don't know how to use those things.

The yogurt shells moistened in the cave of my palm. I loose-tugged my seed-bead necklace. Alexis was standing across the table in her soccer sweatshirt. I knew, I don't know how, that I needed to get her to not walk away.

I said, Do you still need someone to take photos? The Pentax was huge on the table between us. It was clunky and ridiculous. I said, You said something about it last week.

She said, Oh my god, you're right. I'm so sorry. It's been hectic.

I wanted to tell her it wasn't that big a deal. Getting quotes from three different printers did sound hectic.

She said, But I thought you weren't interested?

I said, I thought about it some more. I said, But if you don't need me, that's okay.

I could easily put the camera away. I could bury it in its bandana in the bottom of my bag.

Alexis said, No way! She clapped her hands. It was a get-pepped-up-for-sports move, the kind of clap a team would make before rushing the field. She said, No, that's great. Totally. Melanie and I were talking, and we really did want to give you something better to do.

I said, Are you sure? I didn't quite believe that Melanie had been a part of it.

Alexis said, Absolutely. What do you want to do—clubs? Candids?

I said, Clubs?

She said, Perfect.

I said, Should I start right now?

Alexis laughed. She said, There's not anything for you to take photos of now. She said, Unless you want to take a photo of me? She leaned against the table and turned and tilted her head as if she were posing for a portrait. She arranged her hair in front of her shoulders, then brushed it behind them. The room really was almost empty. I put a yogurt raisin in my mouth and bit: the sweet, grainy outside, the chewy center. Did she really want me to take her picture?

Alexis shrugged and straightened up. She said, Anyway. She said, We need someone to shoot Help the Homeless next month. The benefit concert? I will totally recommend you for that.

The yogurt coated my mouth like paste. I said, Okay. Was she saying that I would do the benefit, or that I might do it? She didn't have time, I got it, to browse old yearbooks with me, or to explain exactly what she'd been thinking when she looked at me and thought Photographer.

Alexis said, There was something else I wanted to ask you.

I'd picked up my scissors without thinking about it. They were open, poised in my hand.

She said, We were wondering. Do you swim?

I said, What?

She said, Melanie and I are captains this year. We were talking the other day, and we were wondering, is Julie Winter a swimmer?

I said, What about soccer?

She said, The season ended last week.

Of course, different sports happened in different seasons, and people who played sports played sports. But swimming didn't strike me as that kind of sport. Alexis didn't strike me as what I thought of as a swimmer.

She said, So are you?

I said, No.

She said, Really? She said, We thought you might. You look like you could be.

I said, I do?

She said, You look like you're built for it.

I felt the stretch of my shoulders beneath my layers—my T-shirt, my henley, my flannel. I felt around her words for a taunt or a trap. Alexis was nice. She said, Let me show you our new sweatshirts.

She went to the front of the room to grab her bag. She took off the soccer sweatshirt she was wearing and pulled on the new one. She untrapped her hair from the hood. In the center of the sweatshirt were two blue squiggly lines and above them a figure reaching, and above the figure it said Jackson and below it it said Swimming. She said, Aren't they great? We convinced Coach last year that everyone wanted hoodies. The sweatshirt was a dark-flecked gray, a real sweatshirt color. It looked thick and warm. The thing about the way Alexis wore sweatshirts was that, even though the sweatshirt was oversized, there was clearly a girl's body beneath it.

I said, I haven't swum in a while.

She said, Do you ever think about starting again?

Maybe I was completely wrong about Alexis not seeming like a swimmer. Maybe she was more of a swimmer than anything else. She was being, it felt like, so honest with me; she was asking the question in a way that felt honest, as if she cared about the answer. I said, I think about it a little.

Alexis said, Really? She said, That's awesome.

My mind pulled for a question about swimming. I said, Where do you practice?

Alexis said, At the Y in Northeast. It's kind of ghetto, but it's fine.

I said, What stroke do you swim?

She said, Mainly breaststroke. I came this close to All County last year. She said the part about All County quietly, as if it were the kind of thing she didn't say to many people. She said, Maybe it's a dumb thing to want.

I said, It's not dumb. The conversation glided. I said, I bet you'll get All County this year.

She looked down and then back at me, from behind her eyelashes, as if although she stood above me, leaning against my table, she was looking up at me. As if shy, but shy on purpose. She said, Thanks.

It felt, truly, as if we could stay there all day, talking about swimming. There were a million things I could ask her about. There were things I knew or wondered about swimming that I had literally never talked about with anyone else before. If she looked at my body and saw it as a swimmer's body, it was possible there could be something she knew that I didn't.

Ms. C. called Alexis's name. Alexis snapped an irritated blink. She said, It's too hectic. I'm over it.

I said, Three quotes from three printers sounds like a lot.

Alexis pushed up the sleeves of her sweatshirt. She clapped. She said, Well, listen. No pressure, but think about it?

The swimming sweatshirt was a really nice one, nicer than the soccer sweatshirt that lay on the floor where she'd dropped it.

I TOOK OFF my sneakers and socks and my flannel. I took off my henley. I dug through my underwear drawer and found solo socks, old shapeless underwear. I took off my jeans. I'd thought I still had one suit that I hadn't gotten rid of, a neon green T-back that I'd probably outgrown but that could give me some sense of what I'd look like. In the swimming magazines the girls' suits smashed their boobs flat, or they hardly had boobs to begin with. My body was whatever it was. I took off my underwear and my bra. I hardly ever looked at my body in the mirror. One day I didn't have boobs and the next here they went. Or there they came. My new suit, if I got one, should have thick straps to break up the span of my shoulders. It should have a long enough torso to account for my height, and it should be blue or brick red. I pulled my low pony-tail tighter. The team suits might have to be a certain color. That was something I could ask Alexis about, or maybe it was something I should just know. I lifted my arms above my head to stretch and saw my armpit stubble—if I swam, I'd have to shave more often. It was ridiculous to be stand-ing around naked in my bedroom.

I got dressed and called Erika. I said, Alexis asked me something today.

She said, Alexis. Which one is that again?

She knew which one Alexis was. I said, Melanie's blonder.

She said, Right. And Alexis wishes she was.

I said, She seems pretty nice.

I still had some of the yogurt raisins in my jeans pocket. I took them out of the baggie I'd saved them in and laid them on the shelf next to the phone.

Erika said, What did she ask you? Did she say she was going to give us something better to do?

I leapfrogged the raisins. I swam one past the other. There was nothing for me to say to Erika about swimming if I didn't know how I felt about it. I said, She asked if I wanted to take photos.

Erika said, Just you?

I said, I guess. Erika went quiet. I said, I'm sorry.

Erika said, You don't have to be sorry. It's exactly the kind of thing I'd expect from a girl like that.

Erika didn't know anything about Alexis. She didn't know that Alexis was a swimmer, or that she had really wanted to make All County and hadn't. Erika hadn't given Alexis the chance to be as nice to her as she'd been to me, and to feel what that felt like. In a way I was still feeling it. I said, I figured if I said yes you could come with me.

Erika said, You said yes?

Later, in bed, my fingers felt around for a good hole in my afghan. The goal was to find a crocheted loop my fingers could snug in, itchy and tight. I found a loop and relaxed and tried to think about swimming. I tried to get my body to remember what it felt like: the push-off and float. The reach. The arm pulling down and around through the water. Through? The little kicks that were supposed to make a motor.

THERE WAS SOMETHING lodged and solid about my friendship with Erika, but that didn't mean I couldn't see it disappearing overnight. Erika and her mom came over for

Thanksgiving. They brought three kinds of vegetables. They remembered my Seattle cousins' names from last year, asked and answered questions, seemed as comfortable as if they were in their own house. Erika's mom wore a long flowered skirt with bells on the drawstring, like they sold at the River Market. She didn't eat turkey, but she didn't seem annoyed that the rest of us did. Erika was usually a vegetarian, except on Thanksgiving and when there was bacon available, as I'd heard her say more than once. If I'd been a vegetarian, I wouldn't have advertised my cheating. It seemed rude to her mom, who I liked, who brought roasted broccoli because, she said, she'd remembered how much I'd liked it last year. I could see Erika and I like spools of gauze unwinding from each other. One of my cousins, who was the same age as my brother, brought his girlfriend. She didn't have a lot to say. She worked for a vet, but didn't seem to relate to Pledge in any special way. Erika said she seemed like a real Suzy Creamcheese. She said my cousin was cute and could do better. I told Erika I thought my cousin's girlfriend seemed fine. If Erika and I stopped being friends, it might be sad for a moment, and then okay. It would be what got called growing apart, which sounded calming, a floating, a benign disintegration.

MS. TRULLI DREW triangles and arcs and straight lines on the board. I copied them into my notebook. I raised my hand for the pass and went out into the hallway. The locks on all the toilet stalls were broken. I held the door shut with one hand and squeezed out a few drops. Ms. Trulli wouldn't miss me. I washed my hands and headed down the stairs, all the way to the sub-basement, a narrow, nestled corridor of music practice rooms and coaches' offices. From behind closed doors came bleats and saws, a flute floating cleanly.

The door that said Swimming/Wrestling/Golf was propped halfway open. It was unclear whether to knock or walk in. A voice said, Someone looking for me?

I said, Are you the swim coach? It was obvious: blond hair a little spiky, track pants, the T-shirt version of Alexis's sweatshirt.

Coach said, Sure am. I told him my name. He said, All right, Julie-Julie. Alexis told me about you.

I said, She did?

Coach said, Glad to see you, have a seat, can I get you anything? Nothing to offer except—a swim team pen? He handed me a blue-and-white ballpoint. He said, Excellent. So you're a friend of Alexis's?

I had no idea what the conversation between Alexis and Coach could have been. It was hard to believe that she'd used the word friend, but who knew, maybe that was the easiest way to describe it. I said, She asked me if I was interested in swimming.

Coach said, Any friend of Alexis's. He said, How can I help you decide?

The cinder-block walls were covered in thick, sticky paint, and taped to the wall above and around Coach's desk were cut outs I recognized as being from Poolside and the other swimming magazines and a few articles clipped from the newspaper.

I said, How long have you been the coach?

He said, Let's see. Three? Four? This would be my fourth year. He said, If what you're wondering is along the lines of Those Who Can't Do, Teach, well— He flipped around a medal that hung off his desk lamp. He said, Go Beavers.

I said, That's okay. Coach showing me his medal was embarrassing. And that wasn't what I'd been asking.

He said, What else?

What kind of swimmer did I need to be, and if I wasn't that kind of swimmer yet, how might I get there? What kind of swimmer was I now? Did Coach know my brother, or know of him? The newspaper photos on the wall were so grainy that it was hard to tell the difference between water and deck. A splash was a smudge. Anyone could have been in those photos. Where did the team practice? How did they get there, and what time did they usually get done? That logistical information was probably printed on a handout somewhere. I could walk out of the office with that handout and know almost everything I needed to know.

I said, What stroke would you want me to swim?

Coach said, That depends. What's your specialty?

It had been years since I'd touched pool water. I said, Breaststroke?

His eyes skimmed my shoulders. He said, I could see that.

I said, I might be built for it.

Coach laughed. He said, Sure, I could see that.

I said, Or something else.

It had been years, and who knew how good I'd be. I didn't want him to think I was trying to compete with Alexis.

Coach said, Well, we could put it like this. You come to practice next Monday, you show me what you can do, and we go from there. He handed me an information sheet and said, The bus leaves at 3:00 PM sharp.

In the hall outside Coach's office the flute still played, or it could have been a different flute. It must have been a teacher's flute, for how unwavering and round its tone was. In this part of the basement the empty halls narrowed like swim lanes. It was peaceful and gutted. If, in Yearbook, Alexis asked if I'd met with Coach, I would tell her. She'd be, I thought, happy to hear it. I wouldn't tell her I'd asked about breaststroke, and I hoped Coach wouldn't, because she'd told me how much she wanted All County this year, and I'd really meant it when I said I thought she'd get it.

I TOOK CRANBERRIES and roast broccoli and passed up turkey—there was only white meat left. My mom said I must miss chicken. I used my thumb to break the condensation on my water glass. Folded in my backpack, in my bedroom, was a permission slip. It had been attached to the instruction sheet. My dad asked how it was going with the camera.

I said, It's good. I said, I'm going to do clubs. Help the Homeless, the benefit?

My dad said, Sounds serious.

I ate a bite of cranberries. I did miss chicken.

My mom said, She didn't say serious.

My dad said, Are you thinking of taking a photography class?

My parents couldn't let me do something without being something. I said, I already have all my classes.

My dad said, What about the JCC? Do they do photography?

My mom said she'd just tossed the latest catalog.

My dad said, I bet we can ask them to send another.

I said, It's okay. I don't need the catalog. The next time Alexis and I were alone in Yearbook, or if she asked me to leave the room with her on an errand she needed a helper for, I could ask her about how she'd decided what stroke was right for her. I could ask her about the pool, how deep it was, and was it clean? And why did we trek all the way to the east side? The JCC was closer and had a really nice pool.

I would tell my parents about swimming, but I would wait to tell them. I would wait until I knew if I was serious. I didn't know how my parents thought of me now—as a photographer, as nothing—but I couldn't tell them I was going to try swimming without having them think that that made me a swimmer. I would wait to tell them until I knew what kind of swimmer I was.

FOR MY NEW suit I could definitely see a dark red, or blue. A navy blue with a sheen to it. Thicker straps would band my shoulders and make them look more proportional to the rest of my body. The black tank top I pulled on didn't produce the sleek effect I wanted. I got out of my regular bra and put on my one sports bra. I put the tank top back on over it and pulled the fabric taut behind me. My boobs stayed pressed flat, smooth as armor.

I put my flannel and my pants back on and went downstairs. My parents were watching a show I didn't care about and I stood in the kitchen. I opened the freezer and looked at the ice cream. I would need to explain why I'd be getting home so late from school. I was going to need to make sure I showered really well after practice, assuming they had showers at the Y on the east side, so I wouldn't show up at home reeking of chlorine. The laugh track sounded. My bare feet were cold on the kitchen tile. I closed the freezer and got the phone books from the cabinet beneath the phone.

Back in my room, I opened the yellow pages. Under swimming, only swimming pool cleaners were listed. The info sheet from Coach should have said where the best place was to buy bathing suits and goggles. My parents knew. My brother knew, or had known, but it was barely dawn in Germany. He lived with roommates and I might not recognize his voice right away, or he might not know mine. I picked up the white pages and turned to the D's. I moved my finger down the page. Of the five

Deitches three had addresses that were possibilities. I wasn't going to call Alexis. It was just interesting to know where someone lived, to guess where based on geography and on a feeling, some faint vibration. My guess was SW 37th or Montview. Montview was hilly and I could see Alexis there, in a house on a hill, in a second-floor window. I picked up the phone and called Erika.

I said, Where would you go to buy a bathing suit?

Erika said, What kind?

I said, An athletic kind. A Speedo, whatever.

Erika said, I guess an athletic store? The Sports Cavern? She said, Why are you asking?

I said, Just wondering.

Erika said, Are you buying a bathing suit? She said, You hate swimming. It's one of your things.

I said, I never said I hated it. I could easily have gone to Sports Cavern at the mall alone—a couple buses, no problem. But for some reason it seemed terrible to go by myself, to grab suits off the racks and pull them on in the dressing room, to make a decision and walk out with the plastic bag. I hated the idea of Erika sitting around deciding what was and wasn't my thing. I said, Will you come with me? Then, because I had to say it, I said, I'm thinking of doing swim team.

Erika said, Who is this?

I said, I'm serious.

She said, I know, you sound serious.

I felt for a good hole on my afghan.

She said, Are you going to say anything else about it?

I said, Practice starts Monday. We practice at this Y in Northeast.

She said, The one on 53rd?

The address may have been on the info sheet but I hadn't looked at it. All of Northeast was the same to me. I said, I have no idea.

Erika said, It's probably that one.

I was ready to get off the phone. I didn't want to answer any more questions. I would tell her forget it and I'd go buy a suit myself.

Erika said, I think it's really great, Julie.

I said, You don't have to come with me.

Erika said, No, I think it's awesome. Swimming is really good exercise. She said, I was just a little thrown off.

We hung up and I got the permission slip out of the notebook where I'd slotted it to keep it neat. I got out a pen that seemed like one my dad would use—his signature was easy, all scrawl. It was one thing to buy a bathing suit. It was another to think of what would happen after. I didn't want to think about it yet. I wanted to wait to decide. I got out of my clothes and the sports bra and put on my best old flannel pajama pants and my softest sleeping sweatshirt. I pressed play on the tape deck, then rewound to the silence before Country Feedback, my favorite song on the album. I lay down in my bed and brought my arm to my face and breathed in. When I dried my clothes with fabric softener they never smelled as good as I hoped they would.

COUNTRY FEEDBACK WASN'T my favorite song on the album, it was just the song I listened to the most. It wasn't even a song, just creaks and twangs and Michael Stipe caught in a conversation with himself. The song had first made me pay attention because he said Fuck in it. I'd had to rewind to make sure I heard it right—a curse in an R.E.M. song? He said Fuck off or Fuck all, it was impossible to tell, and it came after a junk-box list of lyrics, words like rusted parts in a yard. Their shapes were specific but who could tell what to use them for? The song scooped something out of me. It was listening to me and watching me in ways it shouldn't. He sang Our clothes don't fit us right. I wanted to know about Alexis and her swim team sweatshirt, how she got it to fit her the way it did, how it showed and hid her body beneath it. It was a perfect sweatshirt. I needed to find out whether the sweatshirt was a prize for winning a certain amount of races, and, if so, find out how many races I'd need to win to get one. I wanted that sweatshirt more than I wanted a trophy or a medal. If my parents asked where I'd gotten it I'd cross that bridge. At the end of Country Feedback Michael Stipe sang I need this, too many times, in a whiny, desperate voice. No wonder the song didn't get played on the radio.

THE FOOD COURT was overrun with families and kids, surprise, it was Saturday at the mall and raining. Erika took a huge, steaming bite of her hot-topped potato. She said, Why don't more things come with fake cheese?

I said, It's just cheese.

She said, You're completely wrong. It's more than cheese. She twirled her fork in the potato as if winding spaghetti. She said, And less.

I was trying hard to be generous toward Erika. She was giving up her Saturday to go shopping with me, and Erika hated the mall, or said she did. It bugged me when she talked about food as if it were a phenomenon. We'd both ordered baked potatoes with broccoli and cheese, and Erika had added bacon bits to hers. The potatoes were delicious, who cared what the cheese was made of?

Erika said, Do you think the ideal thing would be to go out with a guy from another school, or would it just be annoying?

There were some skaterish guys drinking milkshakes a few tables over. I said, Doesn't it depend more on the person than the school they go to?

Erika said, Obviously. At first glance I didn't recognize any of the skaters from the fountain. I didn't want to look harder.

The stores spidered out from the food court in all directions. Sports Cavern was way at the end of one of the spider legs. It was one of the stores with its own door to the parking lot. It was stadium-lit, way brighter than a cavern, as if shopping for sports gear was the same as playing sports. Erika said, I like that we're coming here to buy swimming stuff. No one comes here for swimming stuff. We're like the underdogs.

Erika was trying to make this into a mission. I said, I bet plenty of people come here for swimming stuff.

Sports Cavern was an amusement park of sports gear. It was like the grocery store with the talking cow. Mannequins acted out sports in frozen poses, and what was it about seeing a life-size doll crouched to take a shot that made me want to touch a basketball? I palmed a ball's pebbly skin as we passed through to swimming.

The women's bathing suits were crammed onto one long rack of limp, flashy spandex. I'd told my mom I needed to buy some new shirts and she'd given me forty dollars. I put my hand on the first blue suit I saw.

Erika said, Oh whoa, 38? I don't think so, Jules.

I hadn't noticed what size it was. And I didn't know, I'd forgotten or hadn't thought to find out, what the sizes meant, if I was supposed to choose the same size as my bra size or if the scale was different.

A store worker in a black-and-white referee's shirt came up to us. She said, Need help, girls?

Erika said, What size suit do you think my friend needs?

I pulled the blue suit I'd had my hand on, another blue one from the smaller-size end of the rack, and, from in between, I took a maroon suit striped with fine gray lines. I said, Thanks, I'm fine, and turned to find the dressing room, knowing there was no way Erika would not be right behind me.

The dressing room carpet had a chemical crunch to it. Erika had been right about the first suit. Because of my tallness the crotch and the shoulder straps held approximately where they should, and my shoulders kept the neckline in place, but below it the chest was a dying balloon, pooching lamely. The bottom of the built-in bra ridged out above my ribs. I looked like someone who didn't know how to dress herself. I balled my fists and stuck them in the gaping bra top.

Blue suit number two was too small to try on over my underwear. I peeled the suit down and eyed the Do Not Remove protective sheet on the crotch. So it was okay for all the people who tried on a suit to stuff their crotch up against the paper, but it wasn't okay if their crotch was touching the suit itself? Or was a person never supposed to try on a suit without underwear? But then why the sheet? I didn't care. I wasn't the kind of person who believed excessively in germs or was sicked out by sharing things, so I got my underwear off and pulled the suit up all the way. If I swam in the first suit, then this one, I don't know, I choked in it. The suit was so tight I could barely stand up straight. The crotch pulled so high that it exposed the white skin where my thigh curved into its socket, and the coarse hairs that sprouted down the curve. I hadn't, I realized, worn a bathing suit since I'd had hairs there. The hairs above my knees were thick and blonde and I knew—from Erika, who else?—that shaving once would mean the hairs would grow back thick and dark, but I hadn't thought about the problem of the dark, thick hairs that sprouted down from my crotch whether or not I'd ever scraped them with a razor.

Erika said, through the curtain, Anything to show me?

I couldn't get out of that suit fast enough. I said, I'm good.

Erika said, Hey Julie.

I was one leg into the final suit. I said, One second.

Erika said, Are you annoyed at me about something?

I said, No. I said, The first two were really bad. I tried to put the sound of a laugh into my voice.

Erika said, Are you crying?

I said, I'm not crying.

Erika said, Okay. I could feel her standing right there on the other side of the curtain. She said, Hey Julie, I have a question and I want you to feel completely like you can say no to it, okay?

I said, Okay. The mirror showed me to myself in the middle-size swimsuit. The suit didn't pull or sag, and it covered what it needed to.

Erika said, Because I know swimming might just be your thing, and I make you do my things all the time.

I said, You don't make me do anything. The stripes on the maroon suit ran diagonally from shoulder to ribs. The stripes took on the path of a cross-current, a potential counter to the strength one could see, if one wanted to, in the broadening pull of my shoulders. Swimming was going to be something—not my thing, but a thing— I did on my own. Alexis had asked me, she'd made a point of it. I didn't even know if someone could just join without having been asked. Erika could, obviously, do whatever she wanted, but it might be embarrassing for her if she went to talk to Coach and found out that the team was full, or that she'd needed an explicit invitation.

Erika said, I mean, the thing is, I like swimming.

I took a look at myself in my suit. The stripes were silvery gray, and maroon wasn't blue but it was, in a way, a color as deep and innocuous. The fit of the suit felt great—tight and enmetaling, a good sling, a shell. I raised my right arm and crooked my left arm behind my head to pull my right elbow. A swimmer's stretch. I could show Erika how to do it. I pulled back the curtain and let her take a look at me.

ON SUNDAY NIGHT I couldn't focus during L.A. Law. It was a boring episode, mainly about the drinking problem of one of the older male lawyers. During the second-to-last commercial break, I stood up and said good night to my parents. There was something—a clipped, vein-pumping energy—that was ordering me up to my room to be alone with it.

In my room I lay on my bed, on top of my covers. It was quiet in my room and my energy was loud. Earlier, on the phone with Erika, when she'd called for the third time to ply me with swim team questions—Did I want to share a combo lock? Did we need to bring towels?— she'd asked if I was nervous, and I had said no and meant it. It was just this energy, a body feeling, fluttering around looking to be fed.

I put on a CD and shut it off. All my music was too calming. I needed something that would match my energy, or drown it out. I put in my one dance album and clicked forward to the bounciest track. The beats introduced themselves and bounced around my room, and then what was I supposed to do? Chase after them? It was embarrassing, for the singer or for me. It was embarrassing, still, in the silence after pressing stop. The phone rang. If it was for me it was Erika with another swimming question I didn't want to answer. I let the phone ring until someone picked up. I heard my dad walking toward the stairs and to spare him the flight, the soft knock, I called, Getting it.

The voice on the phone said, Julie! I hope it's not too late. The voice said, It's Alexis, did your dad tell you? I hope it's not too late. I thought you might have your own line.

I blinked a few times. I sat down on my bed. I said, I have an extension. I said, It's not too late.

Alexis said, I just wanted to check in and make sure you had all the info about tomorrow.

I said, Coach gave me the sheet.

Alexis said, Oh good, I figured, I just wanted to make sure. She said, I mean, most of the stuff is obvious, anyway.

I wanted to ask how she had gotten my number. I wanted to ask because I wanted to know how she had gotten it. To think of Alexis turning the thin phone book page and running her finger down the W column until she got to a number that, she guessed, was mine made me feel something. It was the feeling of running my finger down rows of names to look for her.

Alexis said, I got your number from the yearbook list. The one everyone signed on the first day?

I said, Right.

She said, You must think I'm some stalker.

I said, No. I said, I remember that list.

Alexis said, Great. She said, I just wanted to call. I felt like it was my responsibility, since I asked you.

I said, It's okay.

Alexis said, I'm psyched to see you swim tomorrow.

I said, Thanks. I said, Me too, and then I said, You too.

Alexis said, Don't forget a towel.

My energy knocked around in me. It wanted something big from me. I wanted to know what Alexis thought she'd see when she thought about seeing me swim. I wanted to know what Coach thought. I strained to see it myself. I made fists and shut my eyes. I pictured the pool at the JCC where I'd done summer swim lessons. I saw the bearded swim instructor. I saw my neon-green T-back with the decorative black zipper. Lane lines and kickboards and the smell of chlorine. I saw a blue field I pushed my body into.

The image dissolved when I hit the water. I couldn't dredge up a memory to hang it on. I'd only taken lessons for a couple of summers. No doubt there'd be people on the team who'd been in lessons since infancy, who'd passed every level, who might have been instructors or lifeguards themselves. Alexis might have been a lifeguard. But a lifetime of training only mattered so much. My brother had started late. One day when he was eleven or twelve, he'd gone off to swim lessons, like any kid, and the next he'd come back with a note from the instructor saying someone needed to get this kid—my brother—into training, pronto. One day he'd gone off to swim lessons like any kid and come back another kid. He'd hatched out fully formed and he'd swum and swum faster. I jumped out of bed and got the slippery Sports Cavern shopping bag from my closet. I dumped out suit, cap, goggles, receipt. I looked at my swim things in a pile on the carpet.

My parents had the ten o'clock news on. They didn't hear me go down to the basement. On the laundry room side, I found the boxes and tubs that held my brother's and my old toys. I opened a box and rifled through stuffed animals. I tore the tape off another and felt through Star Wars figures and clumped Barbie hair. The dehumidifer's hum wombed the basement in white noise. I unlidded a tub that said GAMES and found a red canvas tote bag full of chess pieces. The pieces clattered as I shook them out into the tub. The red bag was soft and worn and had the logo of my brother's club team on it. I brought it under the bare lightbulb by the washer. Along the bottom of the bag, where wet suits had rubbed, some of the red dye had leached out, and the color was verging on pink.

I ran up the basement stairs and up the house stairs and at the top of the stairs I wanted another set of stairs to run up. I went into my room and hung the red bag on the knob of my closet door. I put on my sneakers. I went downstairs and got my jacket and told my parents I was going for a walk. I said I wouldn't be long. I said I wanted a little fresh air. The air outside was cold and wet and I turned left and headed uphill. Once I'd passed the houses of the neighbors I knew I started running. My shoes slapped the wet street. I wanted another, louder sound to swarm and match the itch I felt, a sound that was a feeling combing through me. I didn't want to be quiet. If I ran all the way to Alexis's house I could pretend it was just something I did, in the night, for training, whatever, this is your house? I wanted to sit next to her. On the phone her voice had had a sandpaper scrape to it and at the same time something warm and pooling.

At the top of the hill at the end of our block I stopped running. In my memories of swim lessons, one person at a time jumped in for a test. The crowd watched from the deck as each person foundered or glided. I put my hands on my knees like a runner at the end of a race. I heaved in breath after breath of cold, clammy air, but not because I was tired from running.

THERE HAD BEEN a time when my dad and I would go pick up my brother at practice. We'd wait in the car and my brother would always be the last one out. He would swing his red bag like his arm was a windmill and he was about to let the bag go and send it sailing. While we waited in the station wagon, my dad and I would play There He Is. A short boy with glasses would come out of the building. A girl with curly blonde hair. My dad would say, There he is! My dad would say, Well, hello son, you're looking a little different today, and I would go pink with laughter. When my brother finally came out of the building, always last, he would lope toward us, unhurried, windmilling his red swim bag, readying it for the launch, and my dad would say, Where? Where? I don't see him. There! I'd say. I'd go pink with frustration.

There! There! There!


MY NEW BATHING suit was bulletproof. I'd known already, from the dressing room, that it felt good for it to feel so tight, but I hadn't known that when I put on the suit and pulled my other clothes over it and looked in the mirror that what I would see would match how I felt. It wasn't about how the tight suit banded my chest flat beneath my shirt—it was about that—but not about the fact of my boobs disappearing. It was how the flattening made me feel: set and armored. Clearly it would be stupid to keep my suit on under my clothes all day, hot and itchy and a pain to pee, but I didn't want to take it off. I looked at my info sheet as if it would tell me something. The sheet gave information like what time the bus came and when it came back, and to bring a lock and, it suggested, flip-flops. It said foot fungus without saying foot fungus. It mentioned hours for the weight room. I could have crumpled that sheet. I knew everything about it. I remembered, no thanks to the sheet, to throw some clean underwear in my bag for after.

My mom was at the kitchen table doing the crossword with her coat on, and my dad was at the counter pouring coffee. I got my mug and my tea bag and water and pressed the numbers on the microwave. The bathing suit was making me stand up straighter than usual. I leaned against the counter and let the microwave paint me with radiation. I pulled my flannel away from my body.

My mom said, Is that one of the new shirts you bought?

I'd had that shirt for months. I said, I got one just like it. I said, I forgot to give you your change. I put my hand in my pocket as if I were looking for change, even though I had had to borrow another ten dollars from Erika to pay for the bathing suit.

My mom said not to worry about it. She stood up to go catch the bus and I had a sudden fear that she would hug me goodbye and feel the flatness of my chest or the outline of my bathing suit through my clothes. I tried to stand the way I normally stood. My left rib cage started to itch like crazy. I worked my hand over to the itchy spot and pressed. My mom never hugged me goodbye in the morning.

I sat at the table with my tea. My dad drank his coffee and read the front page. He had the paper tilted up so I could see the text on the back, the continuation of an article about the guy who was being charged with murder for giving AIDS to a girl he'd had sex with. Obviously if he knew he had AIDS he shouldn't have had sex with her without a condom, or, I couldn't remember exactly how it worked, he shouldn't have had sex with her at all, but something felt off to me about convicting him of murder when AIDS was going to kill him anyway. I dipped my tea bag up and down and the brown water whorled. My dad folded the paper to the next page. I scratched my rib cage. I said, I might be home late a few days this week. I said, Maybe most days. Yearbook's getting really busy and they want me to stay after school.

My dad said, Taking photos?

I said, Yeah. And other things. I sipped my tea down to the bitter bottom of the cup. I wasn't sure about what to do with my wet hair. Maybe there was a blow-dryer at the Y. If my hair was still damp I could wear a hat and get into the shower as soon as I got home. It wasn't unheard of to shower at night. Pledge ran up and stood shivering on the patio. I got up to let her in and stood for a minute looking out through the glass. Beyond the patio, the grass on the lawn shone with crystalline tips. Somewhere else those tips might bode snow but here they just meant cold rain, colder air.

I said, Do you want to know something funny? It just got cold out, and today the swim team starts practicing. I said, Erika told me. She's swimming this year.

My dad said, Oh yeah? I didn't know Erika was a swimmer.

I said, She's not. She's just trying it to see if she likes it. I said, If you see her don't make a big deal about it, okay?

The sky was thick and chalky white, so dense with fog I couldn't see the mountain.

IN MATH CLASS I felt the sac of my bladder push taut. I should have skipped my morning tea. I'd had to pee since midmorning but I didn't want to deal with the mechanics of getting my suit down. I could leave it up and pull the crotch aside, but I didn't want to stretch out the suit before I'd used it. I paused between classes at the girls' room door. I looked down at myself, pretending I was looking at the floor. My chest really was completely flat. I had to pee so badly but I didn't want to take the chance. I'd seen it happen, freshman year—a girl was at the mirror putting on lipstick and this scrawny, boyish rat-girl came in and the girl with the lipstick, said Oh my god, this is the girls' room, and the rat-girl squeaked out, ridiculous, I'm a girl! I'd been washing my hands. I hadn't said anything. It was embarrassing for everybody.

In Yearbook Erika told me that she'd gone down to Coach's office to make sure it was okay if she came to practice. She said she'd mentioned my name and Coach had said, Any friend of Julie's.

Erika said, He's so nice. She sliced out a caption and said, I didn't know you knew him so well.

I said, I don't. I wondered if Coach had said Erika's name twice, bounced it like a ball. Her name would be awkward to say twice like that. I said, What stroke did you tell him you wanted to swim?

Erika said, He didn't ask.

I said, He was probably busy. He'll probably just see what you're good at today.

It was hard to talk and cut captions neatly, to keep the corners crisp and a uniform border of white around the words. It was harder when I was also keeping an eye on the front of the room. Alexis should know that Erika had decided to join on her own, that she hadn't been asked by me, or anyone, that I hadn't dragged her along because I needed a buddy.

Erika was in the bathroom when Alexis and Melanie came up to me. Alexis said, Sorry again for being a stalker. Your dad must hate me for calling so late.

I said, He doesn't care. I said, Thanks for reminding me about the towel.

Melanie said, Oh, that's good you told her. You can't blow-dry your hair at the Y. We've tried. Under the hand dryer thing?

Alexis said, That thing sucks.

Melanie said, Or blows, and she and Alexis laughed. They laughed harder than the pun called for. They were laughing, clearly, about actual blow jobs, not just the idea of them. I waited out their laughter. If I had laughed as hard as Melanie and Alexis were laughing, I might have peed my pants. Melanie reached into the pocket of her sweatshirt. She said, Dried apricot? She said, Take more. The apricots felt like wrinkled skin. Melanie said, We're really psyched to have you on the team. It was such a great coincidence that you were in Yearbook so we could track you down.

I looked at Alexis, to see if she agreed with the idea that she and Melanie had tracked me down together. Alexis gave me the shy-on-purpose smile. I might have blushed. It seemed to me, just a feeling, that it was Melanie who'd given the blow job.

Melanie said, We're psyched to see you swim. I shrugged. Melanie and Alexis laughed. I allowed myself a micro laugh. Melanie said, She's so modest.

Alexis and Melanie went back to work and I laid out the four dried apricots on the table in front of me. Erika, falling into her chair with an exaggerated sigh— she was so sick of captions—said, Where did you get those?

I said, Melanie was giving them out.

Erika said, Were they talking to you about the team? Did you tell them I joined? She said, Do you think they'd give me apricots, too? She was clearly making fun of it, of them and of the apricots and of them giving the apricots to me. Erika leaned conspiratorially close. She said, I think swimming is going to help us out in Yearbook.

I said, You can have my apricots.

We had a lot of cutting left to do. We'd moved on to the News in Review, a section no one cared about. Anyone who wanted to look at a yearbook just wanted to look at pictures of themselves and their friends. There was nothing on my News in Review sheet about the AIDS guy getting charged with murder. It was too recent. It wasn't big enough news. The title of the article I'd seen was AIDS as a Weapon. That just seemed like the wrong way to think about it. AIDS as a Weapon made me picture a blade strapped to the guy's dick and the guy swinging his dick-blade around. A girl reaching through a guy's open fly and the teeth of the zipper clamping down on her wrist. In health class they were unclear about whether someone could get AIDS from a blow job, or they'd told us the medical research was unclear. The caption I was cutting said Balkan War Escalates. Having to pee so badly made me nauseated.

Erika said, Shit. She said, Can you fix this? She passed me a strip where she'd grazed off the bottoms of the letters. The sliver she'd saved was too small to glue back.

I said, You'll have to print out another copy. I said, Just so you know, there are no blow-dryers at the Y.

Erika tried to press the parts back together. She said, Crap. She said, Where?

IT WAS RAINING, a bored drizzle, as if the sky couldn't care enough to rain harder. The contents of my swim bag were surely dampening. Coach stood at the bus door, clipboard in hand, with a greeting for everybody—a fist-bump, a handshake, a nod. He could have taken faster attendance, if that's what he was doing, by loading us onto the dry bus and consulting his clipboard there. People didn't seem to mind. They stood as if they weren't freezing, as if their towels and swim things weren't getting wet. Alexis and Melanie were near the front of the line. I kept an eye on Alexis so if she turned around to check that I'd gotten there okay I could make it easy for her to find me.

At the bus door, Coach shook my hand. He looked me in the eyes and said, Julie-Julie. You ready?

The bus smell was familiar—plastic and exhaust, body odor. Alexis, from the rowdy back of the bus, called, Julie, you made it! She was with Melanie and some guys. I waved. I stepped into a two-seater about halfway back.

Erika took the aisle to my window. She said, Weird how they love you.

I said, They don't love me. The guys Alexis was with weren't particularly cute. They were regular guys in white hats. They looked like they should be headed to football, or baseball.

Erika said, I don't think Coach remembered my name.

I said, He remembered.

Erika said, I'm pretty sure he didn't. I just told him.

I said, You told him?

I could see it, and was glad I hadn't: Coach trying to move on to the next person and Erika chirpily offering her name without being asked for it.

The bus was hot. Breath fogged the windows and sweat filmed my skin beneath my suit. My need to pee had become a dull, comfortable throb. It had always been easy for me to fall asleep on buses—the hum of the crowd, the lull of the motor. Coach bounded on board. He said, All right! He stood next to the driver, a lightning bolt in a white shiny sweatsuit with blue stripes down the sides. He gave the driver the thumbs-up and the driver levered the door closed. Coach said, I am psyched for this season. Are you psyched? The back of the bus and Erika and everyone cheered and whistled. The cheers braided into a din and I cushioned my elbows on my swim bag. If I leaned my head against the window I'd be out in an instant.

I woke up to a view of the river. I didn't know, for a minute, where we were. We were on one of the bridges heading west to east. I cleared the window to see more. Through the rain, everything was the same color, the river and the sky and the other bridges.

Erika said, Hey sleepyhead. I can't believe you fell asleep. She said, My dad lives super close to here.

I had no idea where we were. The east side meant next to nothing to me. My mouth was metallic from napping, and my bladder felt ready to burst. We passed a community college and a Vietnamese restaurant with the E dimmed out on the OPEN sign. Erika said, Oh, my dad and I ate there once. I asked how it was and didn't listen to the answer. I felt a webless sense, a slipping downward. Maybe it was the murk of waking up from my brief, deep nap to a landscape that was utterly unfamiliar. People talked about the east side, Northeast especially, as if it were a place they'd never have a reason to go—kind of ghetto, like Alexis had said, though I wouldn't have said it that way. I never visited Erika at her dad's house, not for any real reason, her mom's was closer, and there was the story about how in Northeast once someone flashed their lights at a lightless car and ended up shot. Erika said that was an urban myth. The people on the street, who were mostly black, must have wondered why this busload of white kids was driving through their neighborhood. Was it dangerous? It was embarrassing. It seemed hard to believe that there wasn't a closer pool they could have taken us to.

The bus pulled up at a dingy gray building. People around me were standing and gathering their things. They were thronging to get off the bus. My bladder felt so tight I was almost airborne. Just one more minute to close my eyes. Just a few more seconds with my head against the window. My red swim bag rested on my thighs. Erika tapped my elbow. She said, Earth to you! and slipped into the line ahead of me.

THE POOLS I'D seen my brother swim at were huge and new and gleamed like science labs. The water, viewed from the stands, was clear and blue, and the swimmers dropped gently into the pool as if from conveyor belts. I remembered my brother mentioning a sauna.

I pushed open the door to the Y. The lobby had scuffed, beige floors and dingy white walls. It had plastic chairs with some white and black children and parents sitting in them. It had bulletin boards with fliers piled on. Somewhere, behind some scratched-windowed door or another, was a pool I'd been suited since dawn to dive into. Alexis waved from across the lobby. She was talking to one of the white-hats. I knew his name. Greg looked up and Alexis whispered in his ear, still hoisting a weak wave to distract me, I guessed, from her whispering. Greg raised a hand and nodded in my direction. Or it could have been anyone's direction, he didn't know me, and I didn't nod or raise my hand back.

Coach stood in his silver-white tracksuit in the midst of us. He said, All right! He told the boys to go right and the girls to go left. He tapped his clipboard against his watch and said, Seven minutes! He could have blown the silver whistle around his neck to start us. He might have blown it if not for the children and parents sitting on the plastic chairs.

Erika and I massed with the girls to the left. I said, Is it weird here?

Erika said, She speaks! She said, Weird why?

She was going to make me lose it. The weirdness of the Y was obvious. If Erika didn't find it weird, or depressing, it was only because she what, knew Northeast so well, ate at all its broken-signed restaurants. She'd probably come to this dumpy Y as a kid.

I said, It's just different from what I expected.

Some girls went straight to the lockers, stashed their bags, and started stripping. The rest of us hovered in the horseshoe of dinged-up half lockers. A few girls were already stepping into their suits, their bare backs curled against the room. Alexis and Melanie stood laughing at something in their satiny bras, as if they stood around talking in bras all the time. I made for the toilets. Squatting an inch above the toilet with my suit around my ankles, I let a day's worth of pee pour out of me. Someone came into the stall next to me. She stepped out of her shoes and stood on the tops of them, and she pulled off her pants and underwear. Changing in the bathroom was too much. It was taking privacy too seriously. It was drawing attention to something more easily accomplished by facing the wall and dealing with it. My pee finally finished draining. The girl next door reached down to pull up her suit. I reached to do the same, and it hit me: it was going to look as if I'd changed in the bathroom, too. Either that or that I'd, even weirder, had my suit on under my clothes all day. Someone yelled, Four minutes! There wasn't time to undress and dress again.

The girl next door walked out first. She was a redhead with bare legs and an oversize T-shirt on over her suit. She had huge boobs, real obstacles, the kind that were impossible not to notice even with the T-shirt. I felt badly for her. There was no question why she was wearing the shirt, or why she'd changed in the bathroom. She was perfect cover—no one would notice me.

Erika was waiting by our lockers. She flicked her eyes over me and I tensed myself for a question. She said, Oh, good. Seven minutes isn't that long, is it? She had her leg propped up on the bench that ran the length of the lockers and she pointed to a spot on her thigh. She said, I feel like I always miss exactly the same spot shaving. Is that possible? A few light hairs sprouted from the spot she was pointing at.

I stuffed my parka and swim bag in a locker and clicked the combo lock closed, like it was the most casual gesture, the completion of a habitual action. I said, Maybe you should draw a circle around that spot before you shave, and then you won't miss it.

Erika said, That is a genius idea. Except then I'd have this circle on my thigh.

The scumminess of the Y wasn't that big a deal. And I wasn't annoyed at Erika anymore. There was some new thing I felt, my energy, maybe, that made me feel generous. It was good to have Erika there with me in the locker room. It was good to have her to walk with to the shower room and, when we saw that all the spaces except one were taken, to share a spigot for our pre-swim rinse. It was good, even, to have her point out that other swimmers were filling their swim caps with water from the shower and dumping them out and stretching them on over their ponytails or buns before they left the shower room, though I might have thought to do that on my own.

COACH SAID, NOW, some of you might be a little bit rusty. The water might be a little rust-colored at the end of practice, ha. Seriously. For some of you, it's your first time swimming as part of a team. Some of you are itching to get in the pool and show me how many seconds you've peeled off your time since last season.

Little hairs pulled at the base of my swim cap. It felt as if the latex of the cap was plucking the hairs from their follicles. My towel, if it hadn't been in my locker, would have made for decent padding between my butt and the metal bleachers. Maybe my cap was the wrong size, or Erika had showed me the wrong way to rinse and stretch it. Coach explained that today was just an assessment. Today was the day for us to get into the pool and do our thing and he would walk around and notice us and take down notes. Then he would look at these notes and make decisions and assign us to lanes by the end of the week.

Erika raised her hand. She said, So what are the lanes? Like, ranks?

Coach said, Good question. There was never anything in Erika that made her not want to raise her hand to ask a question, even if it was a question she could have easily asked me. Coach said, To answer your question, yes. And no. Typically we've got the fastest swimmers in Lane One, and so on down to Lane Six. But nothing's set in stone. Water—it's the opposite of stone. Water moves.

Normally this sort of hokey cheerleading, this chummy waffling, would have won an eye roll from Erika, but she was rapt to Coach. Everyone was, as if they didn't know that Lane One only ever meant Lane One, and so on down to Lane Six. Coach finished his speech and everyone hooted and clapped and clambered off the bleachers to get in the water for the so-called assessment. Already diving into Lane One were Alexis and Melanie and a few sleek, aloof strangers who were clearly pros, translucent in the water, and already clumping uncertainly at Lane Six were freshman, scared gangly sinkers. The redheaded girl from the bathroom in the T-shirt stood on deck, talking to Coach.

Erika said, He's not going to let her wear that T-shirt, and, sure enough, Coach walked away and the girl set her jaw and lifted the T-shirt over her boobs, let the shirt drop on the tile. She stood there for a minute, glaring at nobody.

Erika said, I'm going to ask Coach what lane we should go in. Should I?

I said, Lane Four sounds good, and led us to the lane-head, pretending I'd known where I was going before I said it.

The water was colder than it should have been. It was colder, at least, than my memory of pool water. I said to Erika, Does this water seem cold to you? It was colder than summer camp water or JCC water. Maybe the Y couldn't afford to heat their water.

Coach blew his whistle. He said, Warm up! 200 Freestyle! He said, That's there and back four times! He blew his whistle.

The whistle, apparently, meant go right now—no time to ask questions or decide the order. People just started swimming. I put down my goggles and suctioned them to my eyes. No time to think about 200 as a high or low number, or there-back four times, because there was the swimmer in front of Erika going, and there was Erika going, and there was me. I took my inhale, lifted my feet, and pushed off.

My body sailed. It flew. To call what was happening swimming would be to render mechanical what felt, in the feeling—the being—of it, like sugar, like a dream. The floor of the pool was toothpaste blue and my shadow was that cool, fast color. My body sailed. My first head-lift to take a breath, already halfway down the lane. Breathe and duck and back under, smooth, there could have been nobody else in the pool. The pool could have been surrounded by everyone—Alexis, Coach— watching me shuttle, sail, unaware of their watching. Something brushed the bottom of my foot and I shook it off and thought of seaweed, as if I were not only weight- less but poolless, as if what I'd felt was the touch of the chorusing flotsam that surrounded and supported me.

I took a stroke, a kick, and the hand tapped my foot again.

The tap was impatient and precise. It was a code: Let me pass.

The T painted on the pool bottom meant the deep- end wall was near. I reached and reached forward, brac- ing for pecks at my heels. I touched the wall and found

descending on me the tapper—who gave a quick sa-
lute, turned, and swam off—and two more behind him,
snared in the pileup. The two slapped the wall and con-
tinued. There-back. I felt fiery. What were they, all three
of them, doing in Lane Four? Who were they but the
types who downplayed their skills to shock with their
prowess, who set themselves up to be big fish in small
ponds? I pushed off, in their wake, but something had
splintered. I slapped at the water. My arms were boards,
my legs were soaked sticks. I pulled hard with my right
arm and almost went head-on with someone—not,
please, Erika—sailing from the opposite direction. I
swiped at the water. The current churned against me
and my breath pulled ragged. I pummeled the water. I
dug bottomless, ridiculous holes in it.

The T, finally, painted on the floor—the flags I
glimpsed when I craned my neck to pull another breath—
meant that the wall was near. The wall was so near and the
water was shallow enough that I could stop and stand and
walk the rest of the way. I hacked one stroke, another, but
why bother? I stilled my legs and arms and let my feet sink
to the floor. I felt the smooth floor on my feet. I felt how
solid and unmoving the poured concrete wall would feel
when I let myself lean against it.

I leaned and heaved breaths against the shallow-end
wall. From Lane One down to Six, I was the only unmoving body in the pool. Lane One swimmers moved
so fast that they became, just a bathing-capped heads
and mouths turned when breathing, foot-soles flashing

at the top of a flip turn. For as fast as they moved, their lane looked quiet. Lane Six was all splashes and separate bodies, swimsuits in colors too loud. The redheaded girl was choppy but strong, easily lapping the strivers and floaters, the wistful twigs she shared the lane with. I pressed myself into the corner made by the lane line and the wall. Swimmers in my lane came toward me and, at the last second, cut a diagonal to touch the wall, pivot, and push off for the other end. Erika was coming down the lane and I willed her not to notice me. I willed her, if she saw me, to see me only as a pair of legs, another goggled face. I willed myself indistinguishable. She took another stroke toward me—Oh, just a leg cramp. She was an arm's reach away—Just a side cramp, just sitting a few laps out. She cut a diagonal and pushed off again.

Coach said, Julie-Julie! He squatted at my shoulder. He said, What's happening?

I said, Leg cramp.

Coach said, Do you have an injury I should know about? The concern that furrowed his brow looked real.

I said, I don't think so. I tensed my calf muscle as tight as I could. I said, It'll work itself out. I'm just going to sit out a lap or two.

Coach, still furrowed, said, Okay, as if he didn't believe I was as okay as I said I was, which was better, in the moment, than the opposite. He said, You'll let me know if you need anything? He rose from his squat and walked away.

At the end of practice Coach gathered us again on the bleachers. He said, We won't do this every day. He said, Now close your eyes. This is just a little something I picked up along the way. I want you all to think about who you want to be out there in the water over the next few months. Think big. Think a Spitz or an Evans. He said, Or don't think of some champion. Forget the fish. Think of you. See yourself as a champion. See you beating your personal best. See you housing that flip turn. See it.

The bleachers were silent. All the swimmers with their eyes closed, breathing, seeing something. I let my eyelids touch and waited for my brother to lope into the frame. All I saw—not even saw, but thought of—was a magic trick I'd had as a kid, a coloring book that, depending where you flipped the pages, showed colored-in drawings, then outlines, then nothing. I opened my eyes. Even Coach was doing it. He leaned forward a little, on the balls of his feet, his lips moving slightly. The pool was placid. The reflection from the high-above lights caught and floated on the water. It rippled and lolled there. I should never have gotten on the bus. Something more, or different, was supposed to have happened. Coach opened his eyes and saw me. He raised his eyebrows and touched his eyes, as if it mattered that we kept our eyes closed for the entire duration of his pointless meditation. I closed my eyes and saw nothing until the whistle shrilled me out of it.

ERIKA SAID, YOU know who I thought of? It didn't seem like something she should want to tell me. She said, Don't laugh. Wonder Woman.

I said, Wonder Woman swims?

Erika said, I'm sure. Wonder Woman is tough. She said, Jules.

It was dark outside already. The bus sat in traffic on the bridge across the river. The roadway tremored as cars moved above us.

Erika said, It was the first day.

Out the window, past the glare of our reflections, was the inky river and lights from bridges. Invisible, un-stopping rain. I said, Coach is going to give me some stretches to do for my leg. Lights swam past the window in the swimming night. I said, Coach said it would work itself out.

After the bus dropped us back at school and Erika took off for her mom's a few blocks away, I stood for a minute by the Elizabeth Street doors watching juniors and seniors walk to their cars. Alexis and Greg separated off from the pack of their friends and walked to a silver Taurus. Alexis got into the driver's seat and turned the headlights on. Montview, or SW 37th, wasn't far from me. Who knew where Greg lived. If she gave me a ride it might be more convenient for her to take Greg home first. The Taurus drove past me and the street was black and shiny with rain.

I touched my hair. It was definitely wet, but it was raining enough that I could explain it that way. I stuffed my swim bag in my backpack and went inside to call my dad. He said he'd be over as soon as he put the chicken in. I took the long way to the main doors where he'd pick me up, past the small gym, which doubled as a cafeteria during lunch. Just past the gym was a trophy case crammed with double-handled cups for football, a plaque with a photo of a kid from the eighties who'd made the major leagues. My dad wouldn't be there for ten minutes at least. In the glass front of the case, my reflection hazed back at me. I had never thought of swimming as a regular sport. I took off my backpack. I crouched. On the lowest shelf of the case, on the right-hand side, was a cup engraved with a silhouette of a swimmer reaching. There was a trophy topped with a figure midstroke, another with a figure perched for a dive. Hamburger grease wafted from the small gym. My breath fogged the glass. There were more gold trophies and cups than the shelf could hold, and they all had my brother's name on them.

BEING IN THE car with my dad was quiet except for the scatter of rain on the windshield and the swoosh of the windshield wipers and the radio newscaster's deep, even voice. I brought my hand to my nose and breathed in hard—the thick scent of Erika's apricot lotion I'd slathered on and a hint of chlorine beneath. My brother had gathered a bunch of the trophies we had around the house and taken them with him to San Diego. I didn't know what he'd done with them after. My instinct when I saw the trophies in the case was to press my hands against the glass to cover them. I didn't want to think about the people who'd looked in and seen them before. My dad turned the wipers up a notch. All I had to say was What happened to Jordan's trophies? or How did some of them end up in the case at school? but I couldn't explain why I wanted to know. What was I supposed to get from knowing that? The smooth-voiced announcer said, Turning now to the Balkans.

I leaned my head against the window. If Alexis had given me a ride, I wouldn't be having to listen to the news or worrying about whether the chlorine smell overrode the apricot. Maybe she hadn't seen me waiting in the doorway. If she'd given me a ride I could have sat in the backseat until she dropped Greg off, and then I could have moved up front. It could be awkward for her to say goodbye to Greg with me in the back. Obviously he was her boyfriend. They might forget I was there and start making out and I'd have to shuffle or cough to remind them. Who knew how far they might go in the front seat of the car, in front of Greg's house, forgetting there was anyone—me—in the backseat. It was possible that Alexis had seen or heard about how many times I'd been passed in Lane Four, and that that had changed her mind about me, made her not offer me a ride. The traffic report came on and the traffic announcer announced that the interstate was clogged, the usual backups between the bridges. The announcer said, The Banfield's doing what the Banfield does. My dad adjusted the defroster and the blast of air cleared the windshield.

At dinner I thought I was so hungry that I took both a leg and a wing, but in two bites I felt finished. Not full, but done. Chlorine itched my skin. I used my fork to pull meat off the drumstick bone. I made a small pile. My mom reached across me for the salad. She said, How was Erika's first swim practice?

I knocked my fork into my chicken pile. I said, How did you know she was swimming?

My mom said my dad had mentioned it. I didn't get why it was such big news. I said, I don't know how it went, I haven't talked to her yet.

My dad said, High school, so she's probably swimming short course, right?

My mom said, High school teams don't have long course pools.

They said the names of swimming terms the way kids who had been to Mexico rolled their r's in Spanish class—over-enunciated, so excessively. My dad asked what her events would be. I said, She didn't even have any idea what lane she'd be in, and my voice sounded mean but I didn't care. I took more rice and salad though I didn't want to eat it. I would have taken more chicken. I wanted to pile food on my plate and waste it all—no saving for sandwiches, no slipping scraps to the dog.

ALEXIS SAID, I tried to call a little earlier this time. She said, Oh my god, first day. I'm going to be so sore tomorrow. She said, How did it go for you today? I meant to catch you after.

I saw her Taurus, speeding off. I said, It went okay.

Alexis said, You're modest. She said, I bet you did great.

I said, Did you talk to Coach?

Alexis said, Oh my god, Coach. He can be such a trip sometimes. Did you know he grew up on a farm somewhere?

I said, I can see that. Coach in overalls, a goofy smile, arm around a cow. I said, Is he always so nice?

Alexis said, Oh, that's right. You've only seen practice Coach. At meets Coach is no joke. He got so mad at a ref once that he pulled the whistle from around his neck and threw it into the pool.

I didn't know if she meant Coach's neck or the ref's, or if coaches were allowed to wear whistles at meets. I said, He's been nice so far, thinking of how he hadn't come over and asked me what was wrong the third and the fourth times I'd stopped at the wall.

Alexis said, That's our Coach. She said, Who did you picture?

I pressed the receiver hard into my ear. I said, What?

She said, For who you wanted to be. When you closed your eyes.

I had been in the middle of getting changed when Alexis called, and now I was sitting on my bed with one leg out of my jeans. I lifted my naked leg and bent it, resting my chin on my knee and touching with my fingertips the light blonde hairs on my lower thigh. I wondered, as I had before, if my brother had been one of those swimmers who shaved off every hair on his body, and if shaving had actually made him faster or had just made him feel faster.

Alexis said, You don't have to answer if you don't want to.

I said, It's okay. I said, Don't laugh. Wonder Woman.

Alexis laughed. She said, Not at you, sorry. That's so cute.

I said, You mean tough, and Alexis laughed again.

She said, You're right, she is tough. She said, You're cute for choosing her.

I felt something—embarrassed? I said, Who did you picture?

She said, Oh, it's boring. Megan Dolan. Girls captain two years ago? She went to U of O for swimming.

I saw Megan Dolan, though I'd never seen her, or heard of her: muscled arms, strong legs, pool-blue eyes like the swimmers in Poolside. I saw Alexis seeing Megan swim, splashless, down the lane. We couldn't take our eyes off her. I said, Oh yeah. Megan.

THAT FIRST WEEK, while Coach roamed the perimeter to watch and place us, I stayed in Lane Four with Erika.

Coach would blow his whistle to start the warm-up or drill, and I'd take off, sail for the first lap or two, and then someone would pass me or I'd otherwise disintegrate. Kickboarding, especially, was nothing but dead end. I'd hold the foam board out in front of me and chop my legs and get nowhere. I'd sneak in a few arm-scoops in order to make it to the far wall and back and then I was done. I'd put my kickboard on the pool deck and press myself into the corner made by the wall and the lane-line, letting the shame burn off of me. The other swimmers in my lane would slap the wall and turn and keep swimming as if I wasn't there. In my mind when they asked me I said, I'm resting.

Sometimes I stopped at the wall for longer than I needed to, past when my breathing had returned to normal, and I watched the Lane Four swimmers swim toward and away from me. It was clear who was really Lane Four material. Lane Four meant average with potential, arms and legs doing what they were supposed to but not particularly fast, or gracefully. One freckle-backed guy in Hawaiian-print trunks kept his head too far down. He should raise it, swim higher on the water, instead of making himself into his own dead weight. The girl I knew from Chemistry could swim backstroke straighter if she followed the lines on the ceiling. I let myself find Alexis up in Lane One. She was good but not as good as the actual pros, who swam so seamlessly they disappeared in the water. I felt as if I knew what that felt like. If I waited at the wall long enough, I could rejoin the drill for the last few laps, and in the starting laps, again, I'd sail. I'd stop for four minutes, three, and when I rejoined the lane, I'd be as fresh as when I'd emerged, lightly showered, from the locker room.

On Friday I didn't kickboard at all—I just didn't. And Erika, who was clearly Lane Four material—perfectly apace, never passed, never passing—said, You know, it's weird. It gets easier if you keep going.

I knew that was a story people told. I said, I'm just resting. I lodged myself into the corner of the lane line and the wall. I turned to my left and saw a twig of a swimmer in Lane Six staring at me. Her swimsuit was pink Day-Glo and she looked around twelve. She was shaking water out of her goggles and she wasn't trying to hide that she was staring. I lifted my arms and did some stretches. For all she knew, I was stopping on purpose. Even if Erika believed the story that it got easier with practice, it couldn't be that story alone that got her to punt herself through 200 yards of kickboarding. She started better. She told herself that story and she started and swam better, swam blind.

At night I pressed my hands to my nose and smelled chlorine. I sniffed my arms and found the crease of my elbow to be particularly pungent. I burrowed my head and breathed deep.

I swam in my dreams.

They weren't dreams about swimming. They were boring dreams where I was doing my day and I'd reach for my jacket from the closet hook and my arm would arc cleanly toward it. I would take a math test and solve a proof without coming up for air. I'd walk from Erika's house to my grandparents' in Connecticut as if the houses were next door and it would be my strong, kicking legs that propelled me.

In one dream I was in the basement of the Space Needle, and trying to ascend it was like gripping a kickboard and not getting anywhere.

In one dream each breath wrapped a thick black thread around my lungs.

One dream was in the locker room. Alexis sat next to me on the bench and put her head on my shoulder. In another dream in the locker room, I overheard Alexis tell Melanie that she'd done something with Greg in the bathroom and I knew the word they used was code for blow job.

One night I was so tired from practice that I didn't dream, or I didn't remember my dreams.

Two dreams were blue.

I LAY IN bed for a while, drifting. It felt so amazing to get a Saturday. My bed felt amazing, and so did my body, which had never felt so completely drained. I didn't get sick often, but the way my body felt reminded me of that—the gaping relief in not being up for anything. This must be how jocks felt all the time. It was better than being sick. It was more honest. Pledge nosed the door open and curled up on the bed at my feet. Pledge didn't ask anything of me but the opportunity to lie on my bed and keep my feet warm. This must be how Alexis, with her year-round sports, felt every Saturday morning, so drained and luxurious. I liked thinking of her lying like me, awake but in bed, in sweatpants, nuzzling lazily into the day.

The phone rang, and I heard my dad pick it up. His soft knock came at my door.

Erika said, Lazybones! I was up at seven and couldn't get back to sleep. She said, Don't you feel this adrenaline? Exercise is amazing.

I said, Are you going to go swimming today?

She said, I would. She said, But we probably shouldn't overdo it.

I said, I was joking. The day I imagined involved reading in bed until I got hungry, and then, after breakfast, watching TV in my pajamas. Saturday afternoon wasn't great for TV, but I could find something. It was too bad I didn't like watching sports. Without really wanting to, I said, Do you want to come over later and watch TV?

Erika said, Today's River Market.

Maybe I was sick. Walking around in the rain looking at the same necklaces and Guatemala bags we'd been looking at and not buying for months was the opposite of the day I wanted, standing under an awning watching skaters because Erika wanted to. Erika said, It's almost Christmas. We should go.

I said, Maybe you should go without me.

She said, Do you have plans?

My bed was a warm glove holding me. Not even my parents, or especially not my parents, made it so difficult for me to say no to them. Erika needed to try actually talking to a skater if she wanted to go out with one. Once she got a boyfriend she'd start to make plans without me. I said, Okay, I'll come.

She said, Oh good, I knew you'd say yes. She said, Don't worry, you're more fun than you think you are.

My dad had a walk in Northwest with his men's group, and he offered to drop me downtown on the way. I was early to meet Erika. Camera World was right there and I went in and dropped off the roll of film from my dad's camera. Out on 10th Avenue, all the punk-rock street kids with their puppies on ropes and their old coffee cans out for change had moved under the overhang of the Galleria to get out of the rain. One asked me for a quarter. He had a cute yellow puppy on a rope. I didn't have any change. If Erika didn't have change she sometimes gave away a dollar. It was cold and gray and already I could feel my thin socks dampening. All my wool socks were dirty. If I'd stayed home I could have done the wash and pulled on my wool socks fresh and warm from the dryer. Buses to places whose names I knew only from the signs on the buses went by with their lights on.

Rich's was crowded, not only with the usual young men and old men but some families with umbrellas, tourists, looking to get out of the rain. A towheaded pack of them blocked the sports section. R.E.M. was on the cover of half the music magazines. It was unlikely, but possible, that they would talk about Country Feedback in an interview. Not that any of their song lyrics made sense, but I wanted, for some reason, to know, not what the song was about, but what Michael Stipe was thinking about when he wrote it. Rolling Stone had nothing and neither did Alternative Press. The radio didn't play it, and no one else who liked R.E.M. ever mentioned it. The song might as well have been a ghost. It might as well have only been on my copy of the tape.

The guy appeared next to me with an armload of magazines. He said, That's wild, I was just thinking about you. He put the magazines down. He said, After you left last time, I remembered why I knew you. Are you Jordan's sister? He said, You are, right? That's wild. You don't remember me.

I said, Who are you?

He said, Ben. I was a friend of Jordan's. He said, No swimming magazines today?

The towheaded family had moved from the sports racks. I could see the covers of the new month's issues. I said, How did you know him?

He said, Just school. I swam for a minute.

I said, You said you didn't.

He laughed. He said, You're right. He said, What about you?

I said, I took some time off.

He said, But you're swimming now?

I said, Yes.

He said, Right on. What's your race?

I said, We haven't decided that yet. I haven't chosen a specialty.

He said, That's cool. Jordan was like that, too.

I said, No he wasn't. He was just good at everything.

Ben said, True enough.

Ben was wearing the clay bead on the cord around his neck, and he rubbed the bead between his fingers. He was wearing a T-shirt of The Smiths. I knew they were a band but I didn't know what they sounded like or what type of person would listen to them. From the look of the photo on the shirt, of a man's bare chest half in shadow, I doubted they were a band my brother would listen to. Still, Ben may have been in touch with my brother and could tell me something about where he was and what he was doing. Ben may have known what my brother had said the last time he'd mentioned me.

I said, So you work here?

It was a stupid question. The room smelled like cigars and wet wool.

Ben said, I do. But I'm actually a landscaper. Work dries up in the rainy season.

He didn't look like the type to be out there with a shovel and a sunburn. He fit right in with Rich's dim light. I said, You should come over and look at our yard sometime. My dad's been saying he wants to do something with it.

Neither of my parents ever talked about our yard, unless it was my dad saying he was about to mow or rake it. My mom had once planted tomatoes.

Ben said, Really? That's cool of you. He said, We could at least have a consult before planting season. Do you know what he's thinking about doing?

I said, Oh, bushes. I said, Flowers. I thought of Erika's mom's wild, loaming garden. She said the eggplant wasn't worth the trouble. I said, And eggplant.

Ben said, Right on. He said, Still at the same number? And then he said my phone number.

It should have felt creepy to hear this stranger say my number, but what I felt was annoyed. There was some kind of brag or claim in saying my phone number from memory like that, and I was sure I had never met this guy. I had never heard of him.

I said, I should go. I have to meet my friend.

Ben said, Right on. You buying that? I was still holding Rolling Stone. He said, You like R.E.M.? You're probably too young to have heard the old stuff. I should tape you some.

Just because this Ben knew my brother, or said he did, didn't mean he knew me well enough to tape me things. It didn't mean I would want a tape he made me. He really didn't look like the type to be out planting in a garden. He didn't look wholesome enough in his T-shirt of a naked guy from a band that nobody cared about.

THE AWNINGS UP over the booths at the River Market kept
the rain out somewhat. I let Erika lead me around. The
incense guy told us five sticks for a dollar. A long ash
hung on the stick in the wooden stand. The guy said,
Strawberry, best seller. Erika bought a few sticks for her
mom. It was hard to make conversation. I kept thinking
about Ben. How he said he'd just been thinking about
me. The way he knew my phone number and acted as if
he knew me. If I told Erika about it, she'd ask me if Ben
was cute. Erika lingered at the wooden bowl guy and I
kept walking. It was more boring to not buy anything
so I got a new Guatemala wallet. Sometimes the white
woman who ran the booth had two girls who were probably Guatemalan with her. It felt easier to buy something
when the Guatemalan girls, who wore dresses in the
same patterns as the wallets, weren't there. It felt embarrassing to give them money for something from the
country they were from, that they or their grandmothers
might have made. The booth next door had these little
clay pots. They were elephant gray, very plain. I picked
one up. I really liked how smooth and simple it was.
They were more like cups than pots. They would have
made a good present for someone. The person at the
booth said, I'll give you a last-day-of-the-market deal
on those. She had shortish, curly hair and a nose ring
and a really cool-looking jacket, like a jean jacket lined
with some material, sheepskin. Jean jackets didn't usually look that warm.

I said, How much?

She said, I could go down to twenty-five each.

Twenty-five dollars felt like a lot for little clay cups. The only people I got presents for were my parents and Erika. None of them would like the cups enough. I thought about asking the seller if she sold the cups anywhere else, so I could ask my parents to give them to me for Christmas or Hanukkah, but it wouldn't be the same if I had to tell someone to get them for me. I wanted someone who would just look at them and know I'd love them.

I wished I knew how to stay standing around the booth without buying anything, just to keep looking at the cups, to pick them up and put them down again, and maybe ask the seller how she'd made them like that, so thin and smooth, and also ask where she had gotten her sheepskin-lined jacket and if she thought it was a place where I could find one like it. Usually blue eyes felt icy but hers seemed nice. I saw Erika coming down the aisle and made what I hoped was a smile at the seller and walked away before Erika got there. Erika asked if I'd found anything cool. I showed her my wallet. I said, Are you hungry?

Under the coffee-shop awning by the fountain was still the best place to eat our noodles.

Erika said, I think I might be over skaters.

My noodles steamed. I pushed a scallion out of the way.

Erika said, I don't know. They kind of seem like assholes. They think they're interesting but they only care about skateboarding. She said, The only problem is they're hot.

The steam from the noodles warmed me. I'd be warmer in a jean jacket lined with sheepskin.

Erika said, I don't know. What do you think?

I said, About what?

She said, Do you think they're hot?

She was looking at me as if she really wanted me to say yes. As if that would make her feel better for liking assholes. I did understand what Erika liked about skaters, whether or not I agreed with it. Erika took a forkful of noodles and blew on it. She blew on it again and then let the noodles fall back into the container. She said, Can I tell you something, even if it might sound crazy? She said, Last night I went to the skate park by my dad's house and was sitting on the bench watching these guys skate, and I decided that if one of them came over and wanted to make out with me, I would do it.

I said, On the bench?

She said, Or maybe behind the clubhouse? Just somewhere. She said, I decided I would let him get to second, but not any further. She said, Is that crazy?

I said, It's not crazy. Raindrops hit the water in the fountain. It was completely crazy. Partly because it was dangerous, but even more crazy because how did all the blanks in a story like that get filled? Something dark swam through me. How did the guy get from skating, to the bench, to sitting close enough to Erika that he could, because she'd let him, get his hands up her shirt? I said, Did you even know his name?

Erika said, Nothing actually happened. She moved out of the way to let a man come out of the coffee shop. She waited until the man was a few steps away and said, The cutest one, though, I thought his name should be Aidan. Isn't that a good name?

I said, Sure.

Erika said, Don't worry, I'm not saying I would really have done something like that.

I felt very small or very old. I said, I know. Erika wanted me to reassure her, to tell her that I had had exactly that same kind of feeling, but I'd never had a feeling even close to that.

We stood there looking at the empty fountain. It was too cold and wet out even for the skaters. A pigeon pecked at a Mounds wrapper. Erika said, Wasn't it weird, the other week, that girl who was skating who looked like a guy? I guess she was a pretty good skater.

The pigeon flew up to the statue in the middle of the fountain. I said, I forgot about that.

Erika blew on a forkful of noodles and slurped it down. She said, You shouldn't be embarrassed. I thought she was cute, too, before I realized.

THAT NIGHT, AS a test, I imagined myself on a bench watching skaters. I imagined one separating from the pack and rolling himself over to me. He was tall and he had hair that fell into his eyes. He said, Julie, right?

and I liked that somehow he knew my name. His lips looked rough. He leaned in to kiss me and his breath smelled like cloves. I focused on that smell. I pushed my sleep-shirt up and put my hands there. My hands felt like paws. They felt warm on my skin. I pushed them around and eventually I felt my nipples get harder and I felt something else, not in my hands or my chest. I let my crotch pound. I didn't know if I was supposed to be me or the guy. I tried to see the guy's face again. It was somewhat familiar. I saw a bead on a cord around his neck. I took my hands out from under my shirt and rolled over onto my side, fists under my cheek, and pressed my legs together. I had talked too much to Ben. I hadn't asked him the questions I should have asked him. What did he and my brother used to do together? Had they been good friends, or just acquaintances? Had my brother ever given Ben something that had once belonged to him, my brother, that Ben kept now in a special clay cup, or wore on a cord around his neck, even when he swam, when he showered? I curled my fists tighter and pushed myself toward sleep.

THE AIR ON the pool deck was colder than in the locker room. Towels would have been nice but it was a thing, for some reason, to leave our towels in our lockers. Coach read out the lane assignments, last name first. Erika, next to me, bounced her knees, vibrating the bleachers. On

the bus ride to practice she'd been all nervous chatter—
how of course Coach should place her in whatever lane
he thought she should be in, but that she really, really
thought Lane Four was a great fit.

Coach read, Berry, Lane Four.

I said, See? I meant it nicely. I meant it to get Erika
to still her bouncing. It got tiring to keep reassuring her
when the outcome had always been obvious.

Coach read, Deitch, Lane Two. Alexis, most likely,
had expected Lane One. I wanted to turn and look up
the bleachers to her, to see if she had a face that masked
or expressed what she felt. I wanted to know, when or if
she called me later, whether to console or congratulate
her.

Coach read out a Lane One and somebody hooted.
Coach said, No verbal feedback. No matter what lane he
read out he maintained the same flat, encouraging tone.
That may have been why it wasn't until the R's that I
noticed Coach hadn't called out a Lane Six. I asked Erika,
to make sure I hadn't missed it. She said, Weird, I don't
think he has. Coach was on the S's. He read, Lane Five.
Every lane he read had Lane Six beating behind it. He
read, Lane Four, Lane Two. The feeling came up in me,
sure as blood. Coach was going to put me in Lane Six
alone.

Coach said, Winter.

He said, Lane Five.

He said it like an apology. He said it like a sheepish
shrug, like palms upturned.

Erika said, Ah! She flashed Coach the finger behind her hand. She said, I can't believe he separated us.

The bleacher dug into the backs of my thighs. I looked out at the pool. Lane Five, as I looked, grew narrow and murkier.

Erika said, It's not fair. I can totally ask him to move me.

I wanted my towel. I said, No. I said, Stay where he put you. You deserve it.

Coach had gotten to the end of the alphabet and he tapped his clipboard against his palm. He said, Some of you, if you were paying attention, may have noticed that I didn't put anyone in Lane Six. The truth? I don't think we have any Lane Six material on this team. There are plenty of Lane Six swimmers out there on other teams, and they're good people, they've got some skills. But I'm going to be proud to say to my fellow coaches, You know what? I've got so much talent on my team that I couldn't even fill a Lane Six.

Coach said, Can I hear it?

I was a quivering line on the vibrating bleachers.

THE REDHEAD WITH the big boobs, Donna, said, You're a sophomore, right? A tiny boy with big eyes and short hair growing long around his ears giggled and said, You're a sophomore! Besides the two of them, Lane Five was four scrawny freshmen girls in Day-Glo swimsuits, including the one I'd caught staring at me, eyeing me from behind their too-tight goggles.

Erika reached across the line from Lane Four and patted my arm. She said, Don't worry, I bet it's only for a little while. I bet if you just, you know, show Coach that you mean it, he'll move you up.

I said, What do you mean?

Erika said, You know. With the stopping.

My hand made a fist underwater. I dug my fist hard into my hip bone. I said, I don't think the stopping had anything to do with it. Coach blew the whistle to start the warm-up. I said, It's not a big deal. You don't need to make a big deal about it.

All up the lanes, swimmers pushed off and stroked. No one in Lane Five moved. The boy waif with his soft-looking baby nipples jumped around like a bird, and the loud-suited freshmen stood bug-eyed and tense. Donna, who'd gotten a swimsuit that covered her cleavage, said, Jesus, someone has to go first.

Everyone was waiting for me.

My arms stroked and stroked and stroked and stroked and my head turned to breathe and my feet kicked. My arms and my feet and my lungs swam me down Lane Five, as far away as they could get me. My legs couldn't do as much as my arms. I let my arms be legs. I could have cut off my legs and been faster. The worst part was thinking of Alexis hearing my name and my lane assignment, seeing me tossed in with this lane of teeming strivers, of tangible misfits. I tried not to think. I stroked and breathed and touched the wall and turned without looking to see if there were swimmers at my heels and pushed off and breathed and stroked. Fuck Erika for acting as if I'd gotten myself stuck here on purpose. And fuck Coach for seeing me founder in Lane Four and not doing what he was supposed to do, which was what, coach me? The worst part was thinking of something in Alexis opening up when she heard Coach say my name and closing off when she heard where he'd put me.

Halfway through the fifth length, my right foot slapped the water. I thought, My foot. My left foot slapped and pulled me rightward. I thought, I'm losing it. My arms went arhythmic. I thought, I've lost it. Down the other side of the lane went a floater, a splasher. I thought, Fucking Lane Five. I thought, Fucking Coach. A striver was inches behind me. I chopped. My hip stitched. I thought. I thought, Fucking Erika, and I knew when I got to the wall at the end of the sixth length—I knew first that I would and then I did—I knew I'd stop at the wall and stay there.

I pulled up my goggles and watched. Donna was the splasher. The boy waif was a feather on the water. He was helpless against the current, and everyone passed him. The other girls in the lane took tentative, practiced strokes as if they'd learned to swim by watching a video about swimming. Swimmers in the other lanes were finishing their laps, which meant that soon Coach would blow the whistle, whether or not Lane Five was done. I'd stopped breathing hard. The boy waif was halfway down the lane in front of me. Before anyone else could join me at the wall, I pressed on my goggles and took off for one more lap, stroking hard toward the little boy. I caught up to him, swiped his heel, and waited for him to shrink to the side.

We had just finished the cooldown and I was about to hoist myself out of the pool. Someone behind me said, Excuse me? Julie?

It was the starer in pink Day-Glo. She was the worst of the videotape swimmers: the most practiced, the strivingest. She said, Sorry, hi, I'm in your lane.

We were standing in our lane. I said, I know.

She said, I just had a question for you, because you're a sophomore, right? I was just wondering, do you know if we're ever going to get to do butterfly?

I eyed the girl. She was scrawny and soft-shouldered. Her hot-pink suit clearly came from the girls' department.

I said, Do you know how to do the butterfly?

She said, I've been practicing. There's a pool at the gym my mom goes to. She said, I thought it would be good to specialize.

Swimmers around us crawled out of the pool. I should have felt sorry for this girl, for wanting something it was clear that no amount of practice laps at her mom's gym would help her achieve. The girl's striving buzzed off of her and roiled Lane Five, where we stood alone, pruning. I felt hungry or nauseated. Beyond the striver was Lane Six.

Lane Six was still, a jewel, and empty.

Lane Six pulled at me. I eyed the girl again, and I could see her getting taller, her shoulders broadening, her triceps or biceps or whatever she needed tumoring up along her arms. My skin felt tight. I was built for the butterfly: tall, wide shoulders, long arms. Big hands.

I said, I don't know anything about it.

I SAID, HEY Coach. Can I ask you something?

Coach said, Julie. His voice, its palms upturned. You know, nothing's permanent.

I said, Actually. I said, I was wondering. Could someone swim in Lane Six if they wanted to?

Coach said, Julie-Julie! You're just getting off to a slow start. It's going to go great.

I said, If they wanted to.

A FINGERPRINT MARRED the shiny gold on my brother's trophy for 100 Butterfly, 1985. In elementary school they'd lined us up in the gym to get fingerprinted, so our parents could find us if we ever got lost or kidnapped. I remembered a police officer, or just someone who worked with the police, mashing my fingertips into the wet purple ink pad. They must have given us something to clean our fingers with. I knew now from watching TV what fingerprints were really for. The print on the trophy looked like a thumb. Ben might have seen my brother win that race.

Alexis said, Hey Julie.

The hallway had been deserted and I'd assumed everyone had taken off, especially Alexis in her silver Taurus, with Greg in the passenger seat.

I said, Oh hey. I stood up quickly, as though she had caught me doing something.

Alexis said, Do you need a ride?

I said, Where's Greg?

She said, He took off. He didn't want to wait around for me while I went up to Yearbook. For five minutes, but whatever.

I had decided not to call my dad for a ride because I didn't want all my calling to make him suspicious. Especially today, when I'd taken a two-second shower in order to get myself away from the pool and out of the Y as quickly as possible. I reeked of chlorine. I said, A ride would be great. I said, Is it okay if I just run up to my locker?

At my locker I put my math book into my backpack. I took it out and put it back into my locker. I needed a minute to arrange myself. I looked in my locker mirror. My hood was up and faint goggle prints still ringed my eyes. I combed my fingers through my chlorine-stiff hair and pulled it back into a low ponytail.

I walked slowly back down the stairs to Alexis. I pulled my hair out of its ponytail in case she thought it was weird that I'd changed my hair in the two minutes

I was gone. Alexis was standing where I'd left her—with her puffy parka and long wet hair and her backpack on one shoulder. Her backpack looked so lightweight and neat, as if it didn't hold any books. Her arms were crossed over her chest and she was a bit bent over, really looking into the trophy case. The look she gave my brother's trophies was dreamy and deep.

She turned and I felt the hologram of my brother settle over me. She said, Ready to go?

Alexis's car had a bunch of knickknacks in it, a little stuffed panda hanging from the rearview, a stack of CDs with cases lying in the ashtray area. The new U2 was on top. Alexis said, Greg said he'd throw the CD out the window if I made him listen to One one more time. But you don't mind?

Alexis asked where my house was. The car was comfortable, the way a Taurus looked like it would be from the outside. The car might have been bought expressly for Alexis, or it could have been handed down. It might have been a rude question to ask. We really only had two topics. I said, How's the yearbook coming?

Alexis said, Oh, it's okay. Ms. C. gets pissed at me and Melanie for not putting all our time into it, but what does she want us to do? It's not like anybody just does one thing.

I said, Right.

She said, Don't think I've forgotten about the photo thing. We're just a little behind.

It would have been a good moment to mention that I didn't really care about photos, and that Erika was the one who really wanted to do them. I said, It's okay. You can let me know.

Alexis put on the wipers to clear a few drops. It wasn't raining hard. She said, So? How is it going?

I said, With swimming? knowing she meant with swimming. I owed her an answer. I wanted to know how much she knew, what she had seen of me. She had been on those bleachers and heard Coach slough me off to Lane Five. Part of me wanted to be so baringly honest with her—to say it was harder than I'd thought it would be and to have her tell me it was fine or how to make it better. I wanted to tell her how I couldn't stop stopping and to have her understand, without explaining too much. But Alexis was the one who had brought me on. She had, obviously, seen something in me, and who was I to tell her she'd been wrong? The heater balmed the air and Bono sang One love on repeat.

The windshield had accumulated more specks of rain. I'd answer when Alexis flicked the wand to clear them.

I said, It's going okay.

Alexis said, Someday you'll have to share some of your tips with me. You must have some good ones.

I raked her voice for sarcasm. She wasn't a sarcastic kind of person. My memory pressed back through all the swimming magazines I'd skimmed. I hadn't been looking for tips. I'd only seen pictures of people who weren't my brother, lists of names that weren't his. There was one page I could almost remember. I said, Think of your arms more like a propeller than a paddle.

She said, Like an old-fashioned plane?

Now I could see the diagrams, like a page from a science textbook. I'd paused to read it because it reminded me of the way my brother swam. I said, Right. To help you get above the water.

Alexis said, I like that. That could be cool, to think of yourself as an airplane. She said, Thanks, Julie. That's a cool tip. She glanced at me and smiled. My brother, racing, was a jet on water. He was a plane never touching the ground. Alexis arrowed the CD back to the beginning of the song. Alexis driving meant I could look at her without her seeing me looking. This was what it would be like to have a sister—driving around, listening to music, talking about swimming, whatever. I looked at her. She leaned her head a little to the left as she drove, as if she were not just looking at the road but noticing it. Being sisters meant an infinity of closeness. I pressed my legs together. Alexis said, There's a party on Saturday. You should come. It'll be mostly swimmers.

My house was coming up on the right. She said, Which one is it? She told me the details for the party. She said to bring a friend. She said, It should be fun? Who knows with these things. She said, Have a good night, Julie, and touched my arm on my way out the door.

IN THE SHOWER I smelled the chlorine steam off me. I worked the soap bar into a washcloth and scrubbed, starting at my ankles and working my way up. It wasn't

redundant to shower when I got home from practice—
the locker room showers were five nozzles, no stalls, and
everyone showered quickly, to save hot water and because we didn't have much time. Some girls took what
they called army showers, sharing a nozzle and taking
turns soaping up, rinsing off. The girls who took army
showers acted as comfortable as if they were showering
at home, soaping their breasts, swiping their crotches,
stepping out of the stream to rub swimmers' two-in-one
shampoo into their hair. Alexis added another conditioner. Agree. She shared the bottle with Melanie and its
smell bloomed down the shower line. It smelled like its
color, a rich, soft green, a part of the forest that got sun.

I wrung out my washcloth and turned up the tem-
perature to scalding. My skin went pink. My body didn't
look any different yet, but it felt different. I picked up my
bottle of conditioner, turned it upside down, and shook
it hard to squeeze some out. Maybe when it ran out I
should try Agree.

ALEXIS PASSED ME on her way to the back of the bus and
said, See you this weekend?

Erika said, You guys are hanging out now? She said,
Those girls are obsessed with you. Here's a Blow Pop!
Here's a granola bar!

No one had given me a granola bar. I said, I don't
know what you mean.

Erika said, Do you think they want something from you?

I said, They're just being nice.

Erika said, I don't trust those girls.

Erika had no clue what she was talking about. She clumped people into boxes and kicked the boxes around. I said, Alexis invited us to a swim team party tomorrow.

Erika said, What does that mean?

I wanted to shake her. She was driving me crazy, and I couldn't say anything. I couldn't tell her I wanted to go to the party. The bus pulled out of the parking lot.

Erika said, No, I mean—do you know that guy Kyle?

I said, The one who sits in front? There was a Kyle who always sat alone, in the seat behind the driver, across from Coach, a seat no one else would want. He wore a black wool watch cap, and he read a paperback book, keeping the cover bent back against the spine. I said, He's going to get in trouble if that's a school book he's always reading.

Erika said, I started calling him PT. For Pale Tadpole. Doesn't he look like one?

I craned up to get a better look. I said, When did you start calling him that?

Erika said, Don't you think he's hot?

He had on the wool cap, and his face was a face. It was pale. He had wire-rimmed glasses and a skaterish haircut, but he seemed more like something other than a skater. Looking at Kyle and trying to gauge his hotness, I felt as if I had never had a feeling in my body in my life.

I said, Sure. I like his glasses.

Erika said, I know, right? Nobody has glasses like that anymore. We watched him take off his glasses and clean them by breathing on the lenses. Erika said, Oh my god. Do you think he's going to be at the party?

I said, I really don't know. Then I said, I bet he might. Do you want to come?

Erika said, I told you I was going to get over skaters.

Out the window was the big red house on a street where there weren't any other houses. The Vietnamese restaurant. An older white guy left the restaurant carrying a plastic bag of food. Erika already seemed so locked-in to her crush, and I hadn't even known it was happening. Her excitement hummed off of her. I loosened the drawstring on my hood. I said, I met this cute guy, too.

Erika said, What? I can't believe you didn't tell me. She said, Who?

I said, You don't know him. He works downtown. I said, But he's really a landscaper.

Erika said, Jules! How old?

We should have still been talking about the Pale Tadpole. I said, I don't know. Ben was old, as old as if not older than my brother. He wore that bead around his neck. I imagined saying, No one has a necklace like that anymore, and having it make me feel something.

Erika said, Where does he work? We should go there sometime so you can show him to me!

I said, He has a weird schedule.

Erika gave me a knowing nod. She said, I think PT seems mysterious, don't you? I like how he bends back the cover of the book like that, so you can't see what he's reading.

ON SATURDAY MORNING Pledge lay on my bed at my feet. My clock radio played the classic rock station. An Eric Clapton song came on. Wonderful Tonight always got confused in my mind with the dead son song. Maybe they started the same way, or they had the same melody. They both started with guitar. In my mind the lyrics or the ideas behind the two songs merged so that Wonderful Tonight, which was the song that was playing on the radio, became about how Clapton's wife or girlfriend had fallen out the window, which was what had happened to his son in the other song. Wonderful Tonight overall was cheesy but there was something that got me about the line where she asks Do I look all right? and he answers so nicely. It made me feel something. Romantic. I could see the woman at the top of the stairs, in a blue dress, backlit.

Pledge jumped up and starting barking and then the doorbell rang. She was psychic that way. My dad's voice and another male voice spoke, and then the door closed and both their voices moved outside. I got up and went to the window and in the yard, patting the shrubs, were my dad and Ben. Ben wore a puffy vest and a wool cap like PT's. He and my dad were laughing, or smiling repeatedly. I put on my slippers and my hoodie over my pajamas and brushed my teeth. Erika would freak out to know that the landscaper had shown up at my house. I put on jeans and regular shoes and looked at my hair.

Outside, it was weakly sunny. Ben was standing by the bushes with a notebook and pencil. He said, I could definitely see you going with some viburnum here. They're good in winter. When he saw me, he raised his hand in greeting like we were old pals. He said, Nice to see you again, Julie!

My dad didn't seem bothered or surprised that Ben was there. He seemed interested in the idea of viburnum, as if he had any idea what viburnum were. I said, I didn't think he was going to call.

My dad and Ben laughed. Ben said, That's what I told him on the phone. But it turns out you guys could use some landscaping.

My dad said they'd come in for coffee in a bit. My mom was out grocery shopping. I couldn't remember if I'd added Agree and cereal to the list or had just thought about doing it. When I was a kid I'd gone grocery shopping with my mom and I'd helped decipher the things my brother had scratched on the list. Every kind of on-the-go food: Pop-Tarts, granola bars, Hot Pockets. My hunch was that my mom didn't know about Ben coming over. Did he have to present some kind of landscaper's license, or did my dad just take him at his word? Ben should have realized I didn't mean it when I said he should call. My mom might drive up from shopping and see them in the yard, imagining viburnum, and be surprised by them standing around like that, laughing on the lawn as if they were related.

I microwaved my tea and poured the last Rice Chex crumbs into my bowl. I dumped Raisin Bran on top of it. With milk it looked disgusting, floating mixed bits, and I thought of Ben coming in and seeing me eating it. I got up and dumped it down the disposal. I sat down and wished I hadn't dumped it.

Ben and my dad came up on the back deck. My dad made a motion for me to open the sliding door. Ben stamped his boots and asked my dad if he should take his shoes off. My dad, in a dad-voice from a sitcom, said there was no need. He offered Ben coffee and poured him a cup. Ben asked if he could also have some water and my dad got him a glass from the tap. The water was cloudy with bubbles and my dad apologized for the wa-ter pressure. He said he had to grab something upstairs and that he'd be right back down.

Ben drank his water first. He downed it in one gulp, without waiting for the clouds to settle. He wrapped his hands around the coffee mug. He asked, Do you drink coffee? You're young.

I said, I drink tea, and hoisted my bag of Lipton.

Ben said, Jordan didn't like coffee. I remember that.

I said, I'm just drinking tea this morning. Ben threw around my brother's name so loosely.

Ben said, What are you up to today? Do you do that whole weekend practice thing?

Ben needed to keep his voice down. Nobody had invited him over here to talk about swimming. I didn't know anything about weekend practices, if they happened, and if they did, how I was supposed to find out about them. Would anyone have told me if we had one? I said, Not today.

Ben said, Yeah, I never knew how Jordan could do it. Total devotion, right?

Devotion was a word from a song on the radio. I squeezed out the water from my tea bag. Ben seemed too at home in my house, at my table, drinking from my mug with hot air balloons on it. I said, Where do you live?

Ben said, Over in Southeast. Near 20th and Morrison.

I said, But you went to high school with my brother.

Ben said, My parents lived over here. But I crossed the river as soon as I could.

I said, Why?

He said, The east side is more my speed. More my kind of people.

I wanted to drill Ben with questions until he disappeared. I said, What are your kind of people?

Ben laughed. He looped his hair behind his ear. He said, Are you trying to get at something?

I didn't like the way he laughed as if he knew more than I did about a question I had been the one to ask. I was just making conversation. I could have been reading the paper and making him drink his coffee in silence. I said, Where do your parents live now? Maybe his parents were dead.

Ben said, Arizona, of all places. You ever been there?
I said, No.

Ben said, I get it, if you like the sun. But it's super dull there. Nothing's happening.

Whatever he meant by that. Ben sat with his hands around his coffee cup as if he were as comfortable in our kitchen as he'd ever been in any room. Ben talked to me as easily as if I were, what, his friend, and he was too old to talk to me like that. He could have been in the kitchen in the past with my brother, but that didn't mean he knew anything about it. If Ben thought our freezer would be stocked with Hot Pockets, he'd be wrong. Everything he said had a wink to it, and he didn't care whether I understood or not. I said, What's that necklace you're wearing?

Ben's fingers went to it. His body got still. He said, Oh, a friend gave it to me. And then he was quiet.

The toilet flushed upstairs.

Ben said, Oh hey Julie, don't think I forgot about that R.E.M. tape.

I said, It doesn't matter. Then, because the way he'd touched the bead made me think that he missed my brother, I said, Thanks. He turned the newspaper around to get a look at it.

I said, Do you keep old magazines?

He said, Some. What are you talking about, music magazines?

My dad came back into the room.

ERIKA CALLED TO ask me what she should wear to the party. She said she wanted to wear something regular but a little special. She said, Something PT will know is for him.

PT wasn't going to be at this party. What was he going to do, show up with his hat and his bent-back paperback? I said, Some kind of accessory?

Erika said, I guess what I mean is, I got this shirt that I thought might be too tight, but maybe I should wear it?

I didn't want to picture Erika in a tight black scoopneck, to see her in it and know she was wearing it to get PT, who wasn't going to be there, to look at her chest. I told her she should wear the shirt if she felt like it.

Erika said, Ah! I'm asking you what you think!

I said, I just told you.

Erika said, Fine. Okay. I probably won't wear it. She said, What are you going to wear?

Erika's mom dropped her off at my house after dinner. Erika was wearing lipstick, or gloss, something that made her lips pink and shiny. She came into my room and took off her coat dramatically. She was wearing the tight shirt. She said, I brought a backup, so just tell me. The shirt looked exactly the way I had imagined—not imagined, but pictured without wanting to. It was impossible to look at Erika in the shirt and not look at her boobs, or the shadow of cleavage the shirt revealed. The cleavage was new to me. It was there—she had made it, somehow, be there. Erika's boobs looked bigger than I'd thought they were. I didn't want to notice that. I didn't want to spend the party worrying about whether people thought Erika looked slutty in her shirt, or whether she felt slutty, standing around imagining what PT's hands would feel like on her. Erika was wearing her matching seed-bead necklace. She said, You were right about accessories.

I had on my off-white thermal henley over a navy T-shirt and my dark jeans. I had a little silver ring I sometimes wore, with a turquoise chip in it. Erika rolled on more lip gloss and offered it to me. I said, No thanks. I hoped Erika would put her jacket back on before we left the house so my parents wouldn't see her tight shirt and wonder why she was dressed that way, or why I was dressed the same way I always was.

It was drizzling lightly and we put up our hoods. A couple blocks away a streetlight went out just as we were passing under it. Erika said, Weird.

I said, It happens all the time.

Erika stopped in the shadow and looked over her shoulder. She said, Wait a second and went into her bag. She took out a flat, wide red-and-white box. She said, Want one?

I said, Where did you get those?

She said, This place on the east side I heard about. Near my dad's. She said, They sell to anyone.

I said, You heard from who?

She said, These girls who were smoking at the bus stop.

I said, And you just went up and asked them? There was a lot missing from the story—like what exactly Erika had said to those girls, and what kind of girls they were, and whether they went to our school. And if they had offered her one of their cloves and if she'd taken it, and if she'd known how to smoke it, and if they'd been rude or nice to her in her fleece pullover and Sebagos. I said, Whoa. All these secrets.

Erika burst out laughing, so hard that she had to stop trying to light the clove she was trying to light by cupping her hands around it against the rain. She said, That coming from the most secretive person in the world. She fake-wiped tears from her eyes. The streetlight buzzed back on and she paranoidly tucked the unlit clove inside her hand. She said, Compared to you, I'm like an open book.

I said, Come on.

She said, An open telephone book.

We arrived at the party reeking of cloves. I'd been better at inhaling than I thought I'd be. I liked the feeling of drawing the smoke down until it crowded my lungs and then letting it out in a strong, steady jet. It felt like completing a sentence. The swimmer whose house it was, who was called, by everyone, Grapestuff, opened the door. He said, Ladies! He stood there with his long arms hanging, expectant, as if waiting for a hug. I said, Alexis invited us. Grapestuff showed us where to throw our coats and pointed us toward the basement.

He said, My parents are home, so . . . He shrugged.

Erika said, That means no beer. That was fine with me. Pulling the clove smoke so deep into my lungs had

left me lightheaded. Grapestuff had a basement from the
seventies, when people made basements for parties and
called them, what, rumpus rooms? Carpeted and wood-
paneled and a built-in bar with bowls of potato chips and
two-liters of soda on it. There was a pool table no one was
playing on. Leaning against it were two of the pro swimmers, a gangly guy and a girl, and another girl who must
have gone to a different school, all wearing their silk All
County jackets. They looked out of place in the wood-
paneled basement, angel aliens on dry land, as if we'd
burn up if we touched them. Erika nudged me. She said,
Should we talk to them? Maybe they want to play pool.

I said, Do you know how? and as I was saying it the
guy pro raised his hand to wave to us.

Erika said, He's waving at you. She was right. I was
who he was looking at. Erika said, We should go over
there. How hard is it to play pool?

The guy said, What was your name again? I told him,
and he said to the girls he was with, Do you know who
her brother is? And then he said my brother's name.

The girl who didn't go to our school looked me up
and down. Her eyes were half-closed and she looked
barely awake. She said, Oh yeah, that guy. She kind of
looks like him, right?

I said, Not really.

Erika said, You sort of do.

I said, No I don't.

The guy said, What's he doing these days? Bummer
about Seoul.

I said, He travels all over. Doing speaking engagements and that kind of thing.

The guy said, Cool, cool. He still gets in the pool, right?

I pretended that Erika wasn't standing right there. I said, Of course.

The guy nodded, slowly, longer than he needed to. Erika, too loud for how close we were standing to them, said, They are so stoned. The two girls had moved around to the other side of the pool table and were clacking the pool balls into their triangle frame. Of course they were stoned. They were stupid stoners asking pointless questions. Erika thought that because she always knew when people were on drugs meant she knew more about people.

Grapestuff was making the rounds with a platter of pigs in blankets. He made an exaggerated, obsequious lunge toward us with the platter, and said, Ladies? Specialty of the house. The pigs in blankets smelled like old hot-dog water. Grapestuff said, You're swim team, right? He wasn't even trying to pretend that he wasn't staring at Erika's boobs. It was disgusting. It was more disgusting to think that she knew he was staring and didn't care, or liked it. I pulled my shirt away from my chest. Erika took a pig by the toothpick and dipped it in mustard.

I said, Those aren't vegetarian.

Erika said, It's the weekend.

I took one because Grapestuff was still standing there waiting for me to take one, and because I usually

liked pigs in blankets. Grapestuff said, That's what I like
to see. He backed away with his platter and said, If you're
lucky, ladies, by the end of the night I'll tell you why they
call me Grapestuff.

The pros had started knocking around the pool balls.
Erika and I found seats on a couch that had a clear view
of the stairs, so Erika could keep watch for PT. The music was Pink Floyd or something, a band I didn't get why
people thought of as deep. It sounded like a music box
under a pillow. Erika said, Maybe you should ask those
swimmers for some pot.

I said, You can if you want.

Erika said, You're the one they want to be friends
with. It's like they think if they're nice to you, you'll in-
troduce them to your brother.

A look must have come on my face. Erika put her
hand on my arm. She said, I didn't mean that.

The look must have just been a surprised look. I
was only surprised because Erika never mentioned my
brother. I said, It doesn't matter.

Someone turned up the volume on the stereo. A
clump of non-swimmer sophomores shouted the lost-
souls-in-a-fishbowl line. Erika said, It's really hard to
imagine PT at this party.

I said, It's really hard to imagine us at this party. I
wasn't trying to be funny but as soon as I said it I knew
it was the funniest thing I'd ever said. Erika laughed and
I laughed until chewed-up specks of hot dog burned my
throat.

The doorbell rang and Grapestuff said, Finally, dudes! and a pack of swimmers tumbled into the basement. Erika said, Your friends are here. Alexis had gotten a haircut, to just above her shoulders. It made her look older, or nicer. Erika started talking to one of the guys from Lane Four. He had glasses that were kind of like PT's. Alexis went over to get a soda and I got up for a refill. She said, Julie! She said, I'm so glad you made it, and put down her soda to give me a quick, light hug. I smelled alcohol, a touch of cigarette and fabric softener. She was wearing her oversize swimming sweatshirt. Who knew what she had on beneath it, but, no offense to Erika, I thought it was a better choice for a party than showing everything off.

I said, You got a haircut.

She nodded and took the ends of her hair between her knuckles and tugged, as if to pull it back to its former length. She said, I'm not exactly used to it.

I said, It looks nice. The compliment came like a cold copper penny dropped into my mouth. It was as if all I had to do was say it and she would, and she did, touch her hair again and say Really? and then say Thanks, and then look at me as if looking up at me before she went back to her friends.

I sat on the couch, playing with my ring and half listening to Erika talk to whoever about things I didn't know she knew or cared about: the Dead, snowboarding. She squeezed my arm every time the doorbell rang. Eventually she stopped squeezing. Alexis stood with her friends by the stairs, leaning against a wall of pho-tos. She went up and down the stairs with Melanie and, once, with Greg. It wasn't even that I wanted to talk to her again, or for longer, or for her to be sitting on the couch next to me. I wanted to keep being in the same room with her and sensing her like heat.

After one trip back from upstairs Alexis and Melanie stood whispering and, it seemed like, looking at me. Alexis whispered something to Melanie and then she made a come here signal with her finger. I pointed at myself, a goofy move, and Melanie cupped her hands to call across the room, Come over here Julie Winter please.

Alexis said, Julie. I'm so glad you made it.

I said, Thanks. Alexis's cheeks were flushed. She had never looked happier.

Melanie said, Listen, we just wanted to ask you something.

Alexis said, Wait. Do you want a sip?

She handed me a cup with Mountain Dew in it. She said, It has a lot of vodka in it, and Melanie said, A lot, and the two of them laughed in a way that shut me out of their laughing. It wasn't their fault. The drink smelled so strong that the yellow of the soda might as well have been food coloring.

Melanie said, Listen. So, Alexis thinks your brother is really hot—

Alexis said, No! We just think he was a really great swimmer—

Melanie said, And his picture in this old yearbook we saw is really hot—

Alexis said, And we just wanted to ask you. What is he doing now?

They said, Does he live nearby?

They said, Do you think he'll ever show up to a meet?

The craziest thing was how calm I felt. Maybe the pro guy asking had prepared me—but this felt different. I'd seen Alexis staring into the trophy case. My brother and I had none of the same features, but, it was true, people had said before that we looked alike. I took another sip of Alexis's drink. It gauzed me in something bold and warm. It was as if I'd been waiting all night, years, to be asked these questions.

I said, He travels a lot. All over the world.

I said, He stays in shape.

I said, It's hard to say when he'll be around, with all his traveling. I'm going to send him the meet schedule.

Alexis said, He must be so psyched that you're swimming.

I said, He can't wait to see me.



ON OUR WAY out, on my way up the stairs, I felt a tug on the cuff of my henley. Alexis was leaning against the wall under the stairs with Greg. She said Good night, Julie, and let my cuff go. Erika and I got our coats and headed back down the hill. It had stopped raining and mist silvered the air. Erika said, That Grapestuff is kind of a dork, right? She said, Those girls were wasted, weren't they? What did they want to talk to you about?

I said, Just some Yearbook thing. My arm was still tracking in the direction Alexis had pulled it.

Erika said, What about Yearbook?

I said, It turns out I can't do photos. They hadn't cleared it with Ms. C. before they asked me.

Erika said, Are you bummed?

I said, Not really. I said, Not for me. If they had given me an assignment, I was going to give it to you. Generosity brimmed out of me. I said, I'm sorry PT didn't show up.

Erika said, Yeah, I knew he wouldn't. She flicked her lighter at a clove and held the lit clove without smoking it. She said, If I can get invited to a party he's going to be at you'll go with me, right?

I said, Of course. It was shiny out. The pavement was slick and the streetlights were starfishes of light. It was so quiet, except for the occasional car revving wetly up the hill. My mind felt foamy and clean. Erika passed me the clove and I took a deep drag. I let the smoke sink down and used the full force of my lungs to push it out.

I COULDN'T KEEP myself asleep. I woke up at 3:30 AM, 4:00, 5:15. At 6:00 AM I realized what it was: I was starving. I had never been hungrier. I went downstairs quietly. I could make eggs and toast but at some point my parents would wake up and talk to me. They'd want to ask me how the party went. I left a note on the counter.

Nobody was out and the sky was dark blue, purpling at the edges. I'd never really seen a sunrise. As I waited for the bus I looked east. The whole sky lightened around me. The bus was fuller than I'd expected and completely silent. Of course people had jobs on Sundays. They probably didn't want to go to them, or talk about them. My spot was sideways-facing, and I sat forward on my seat to avoid touching, or crowding out, the people next to me. It was peaceful on the bus. It was nice how people called Thank you to the driver when they got off. Downtown looked quiet and clean, a movie set of a city. I was so awake.

Mar-Shell's was the only 24-hour diner downtown. Still left downtown, my dad would say. I had good memories of coming for weekend breakfast and choosing songs from the jukeboxes that sat on each table. Sometimes, if it was after practice, my brother would be with us. The joke was that my mom would always choose Total Eclipse of the Heart after flipping through the songs and acting as if she might choose something different. I sat at the counter and ordered a two-egg breakfast and a cup of tea. I was definitely the youngest person in the diner. Nobody seemed to notice, or care. There was no need for me to come up with a story, other than that I'd woken up early and been ravenous and wanted to eat eggs at a diner. I had some money, why wait? There were other people at the counter eating alone, and groups in the booths. Some of them might have been out all night. I could tell from their clothes, and they seemed wound up, on the far side of tired. In a booth by the windows was a guy with his head on another guy's shoulder. They had their fingers intertwined between their plates on the table. The waitress didn't say anything or act weird when she refilled their coffee. I knew that in New York and San Francisco and maybe here they had bathhouses with rooms for sex in them. Maybe all the rooms became sex rooms at some point. Not that I knew anything about it, but that didn't seem like what those guys had been doing all night. I mashed up my eggs with my potatoes and ate everything on my plate. I sopped up the yolk with my butter-soaked toast.

I needed to pick up my film from Camera World, which had been ready in an hour but had been sitting there for weeks. The store wasn't open yet. It was funny how when a store was open it seemed as if it had always been open and would be until closing time. But who thought about the mornings? I felt warm with tea and greasy potatoes, and it might have been a figment but I felt that something had happened between me and Alexis at the party. The only way I could understand it was that she felt it, too. Half a block down, Rich was rolling up his grate. I took a weekly newspaper from the box and leaned against a building. They were making plans for a new central library but hadn't factored in enough room for all the books. Now they had to figure out whether to change the plans or get rid of some of the books. I thought of Ben saying Arizona was super dull. I'd meant to ask him what his schedule was so I could avoid going into Rich's when he was working. It seemed unlikely that he'd be working so early on a Sunday.

I pushed the door open and the bells jingled. Rich came out of the back room, saw it was me, and told me to holler if I needed anything. He said, I can trust you, sweetheart, right? I felt a little bad that I never bought anything. I picked up Swimming Monthly. My brother had covered the walls of his room with pages ripped out of these magazines. There was something about that that seemed more honest than putting up pictures of bands or movie stars. It was better than mirrors, the image of the thing he wanted to be. What did it feel like, the day he opened a magazine and saw a glossy picture of himself?

I put the magazine back and went up to the register. The red-and-white boxes of cloves had their own section in the stacks of cigarettes behind the counter. I picked up a pack of Trident and waited for Rich to come out of the back room.

THE WISPY BOY disappeared from Lane Five. It was as if the current had taken him. I kicked. I stroked. I tried to keep my elbow lifted. I tested and sorted the reeds of myself, and I could feel something happening. My body knew what it was doing. I stuffed a pull-buoy between my thighs and my arms were golden. Water moved for me. I went arm to pit to hip to toe and I let my mind catch on moments: Alexis calling me over. Alexis pulling at my cuff. My memory rubbed the moments raw.

In the middle of the 200 Back I bumped into the striver and she told me I'd swim straighter if I followed the lines on the ceiling. I said, I know that.

At the end of the length I rested my elbows on the wall's metal lip. Donna swam up and stared at me. She said, What's up with you?

I said, What do you mean?

She said, Not to be rude, but why do you stop after every lap?

I said, I'm just resting. I said, It's not every lap. I get leg cramps. You can ask Coach.

Donna said, No offense, but if you don't want to be here, you shouldn't be.

She looked as if she might punch me. Not at that moment, but later, when she wasn't in her bathing suit, and when there weren't swimmers around to witness it.

I said, It's fine.

She said, Not really.

I said, It's fine.


MY DAD WAS finishing up a work project and couldn't come get me after practice. I lingered for a minute at the trophy case. Nobody came up behind me. At the bus stop an old woman said the 47 had just passed. The time it would take for the next one to come would be longer than it would take me to walk home. The rain was steady and light, strong enough to notice but not to care about. At the corner ahead a silver Taurus pulled up at the curb, U2 was playing loud. Greg leaned out the passenger window and asked if I wanted a lift. I told him I was almost home. Alexis, from the driver's seat, asked if I was sure. She said, It's raining.

I said, It's okay, I like walking. It was cold and dark and wet and late.

On my front lawn was a wheelbarrow with a tarp over it. I looked under the tarp: wood chips. Some space had been cleared in front of the house, and I couldn't remember what had been there before. Next to the wheelbarrow were a few small bushes swaddled in burlap. The cleared space made the house look naked.

At dinner I said, What's going on with the front of the house? My dad said Ben had had the day off so he'd decided to get started. He'd brought in some plants that would do well through the winter.

Our old plants had done fine through the winter. Ben was becoming some kind of lurker, hanging around when I wasn't there. I didn't want him around when I wasn't, digging holes in the yard with my dad standing by. I could see them, Ben leaning on a shovel, my dad in his raincoat. It wasn't crazy to think Ben might have asked where I was, or what time I got home from practice. I said, What did you guys talk about?

My dad said he'd been busy working, that he hadn't really had the time to chat. I said, Then how did he know where the plants should go? My dad said he'd trusted Ben to figure it out. I didn't know what reason my dad had to trust him. I got up to get a new bottle of salad dressing from the refrigerator. On the door was a magnet for USA Swimming that had been there forever, so old it couldn't hold anything up. Had my brother stuck it there or had my parents put it up in hopes he'd notice?

I got the bottle from the fridge and stood there holding it. I said, I joined swim team. I said, I thought I should tell you before you found out from Ben.

My mom said, Ben?

I didn't know why I had told Ben. I said, I'm sorry I didn't tell you before.

My mom said, Well, we're not shocked.

My dad said, We had a feeling.

I wasn't telling them to shock them. I said, You had a feeling when?

He said, When you told me about Erika.

I felt myself getting angry. The angry feeling flared over something else. I said, Then why were you asking me how Erika was doing?

My mom said, We wanted to give you the opportunity to tell us on your own.

They'd gummed me up in a trap. I waited for them to get mad, to ask why I hadn't told them. My dad reached for the last drumstick.

I said, Do you want me to tell you anything else about it? I waited for them to ask what events I was swimming, and how good I was. I wouldn't tell them about stopping, but I'd describe how I swam just after stopping, when the machine of my body worked best.

My mom said, What else do you want to tell us?

I said, Nothing.

I made myself watch a little TV with my parents after dinner and I got up at a commercial to get a snack. This felt like Ben's fault. In the front of the Rolodex was a business card with a green background and a small graphic of a crossed rake and another garden tool, and above it it said Benjamin Mitchell, Landscaping and Yardwork. In quotes it said Competitive Rates. My parents were probably overpaying him. I took a sheet of scrap paper from the grocery-list pad and wrote down the address and phone number from the card. I didn't write anyone's name on it. I folded the paper and put it in my pocket.

ALEXIS GAVE ME a strip of her Kit Kat. Melanie offered me some gummy bears. Erika said I could get rich starting a resale business, with all the treats they gave me. She said she'd passed PT in the hall and he'd said Hey, and the next time the two of them were thrown into a circumstance like that, she was going to keep the conversation going. I said she could go sit with him on the bus if she wanted to. She said sitting with him would be like entering his inner sanctum.

Our opening meet was a week away. I was the first to take off for the first drill, without anyone asking me to, practically before the whistle blew, and I swam as hard as I could to get some distance between me and the rest of my lane. Coach was walking around with his clipboard. He'd watch us and let us know our races on the day of the meet. I lifted my head higher. Looking ahead made my body feel lighter. I slapped the wall and turned quickly. Freestyle was the stroke that made the most sense to me—my arms pulling water, my legs more or less kicking to propel me. 50 or 100 Freestyle was something I could more than handle. After eight lengths I stopped at the wall.

The striver sidled up to me before Coach called out the cooldown. She said, Can I give you a little tip?

I said, What?

She said, Your head? You shouldn't hold it up quite so much. It spoils the line?

I said, What?

She said, The line? That your body's supposed to stay in when you swim. It sounded like something from a textbook about swimming. What did she do, read up at night and memorize tips? She said, What race do you hope he puts you in? I'm really hoping for 100 Breast. Or a breast spot in the Medley Relay.

On her cheek was a whitehead shiny with pus. I said, I thought you were into the fly.

She said, I changed my mind, after you talked to me about it. She said, What do you think my chances are?

I wanted to say, Why are you asking me?, but I knew why.

Coach called me over on my way to the locker room. If he asked me what race I wanted to swim, I'd say 100 Free. I wouldn't tell Erika he'd asked me, because she wanted so badly to swim 100 Back, the same race as PT. I'd save her from knowing I'd gotten to choose and she hadn't.

Coach said, I found this in my files. Thought you might want to take a look.

The pamphlet said Miracle Swimming. The smaller print said How to Feel Safe in Deep Water. I said, I'm not afraid of the water.

Coach said, Sure.

I said, You see me swimming in there every day.

Coach said, Right. I was thinking about this part. He took the pamphlet back and pointed to a heading that said Panic Prevention. He said, Believe it or not, I was there once. I had these little pink pills I would take.

The pamphlet said when panic came to take deep breaths and count back slowly from ten. It had nothing to do with me. I said, I'm not panicking. I get cramps.

Coach said, Sure. Same story with me.

The pool deck was freezing. I hated that my towel was in my locker. I said, Why don't you just cut me?

Coach said, That's not in my philosophy.

I got my swim bag out of my locker and stuffed the

pamphlet in the bottom. I didn't want to risk throwing it in a can where anyone could find it.

THE CLASSIC ROCK station was coming in staticky. I moved my arm toward the dial and the signal got clearer. I dropped my arm on my pillow and the fuzz came back. My body felt dead. I put the back of my hand to my forehead. Coach was so full of shit, the way he thought he was helping me out. Handing me that pamphlet was him tossing me in a hole and saying, Swim out of it. Or saying I was already in a hole and he was sorry but he didn't know if I could swim out of it. He hadn't said he was sorry.

Pledge's body warmed my feet. Any minute she would start barking and the doorbell would ring and Ben would be there in the yard, digging holes. If I had the energy or desire to get out of bed, I would put on R.E.M., loud, and time it so that Country Feedback was playing when Ben came in for his coffee. Then he would get over his idea that I only liked the same songs everyone liked. I wanted to see the look on Ben's face when I told him I was going to quit. I wanted to see him awkwardly figuring out what look to throw on. He'd been so self-satisfied when I told him I was swimming, so sure he'd known from the first time he met me. He thought he knew me better than I knew myself.

Pledge jumped up and started barking and it was my mom coming back from grocery shopping, and I got up and put on a hoodie and slip-ons. I wanted to see if she'd gotten the Hot Pockets I'd put on the list.

My dad was outside pushing wood chips around. My mom said she thought the landscaper was supposed to take care of that. My dad said that Ben had been called in to his other job and couldn't make it until next week. My mom said if the project got left halfway done, she wasn't planning to be the one to help finish it. She was right to be pissed off.

I said, I'm not helping either.

He used the back of his work gloves to sop up his sweat. I thought he was going to tell us Ben was fired. He said he was glad to know he could count on us. He held his back as he stood up, a comic-book version of an old man straightening. He was too old to be doing yard work.

TWO BUSES THAT weren't mine came first. Nothing felt stupider than stepping up to the curb and raising my hand to make the driver stop, and then realizing that it wasn't the 47. The jumpy guy in a running suit bouncing his knees in the bus shelter said, Fucking buses. His accent sounded like something. When the 47 came he stood behind me in the aisle. He looked like Baryshnikov. He hadn't shaved, or he couldn't grow a real moustache. He was wearing an outfit Coach might wear, but he didn't remind me of Coach. Once he reached into his pants and adjusted, or whatever it was guys did when they did that. I thought, after the adjustment, that I could make out the edge of something pushing against the shiny fabric. The guy was wearing cologne. He cracked his knuckles and stared at nothing. If he were a coach of something, he would be a mean coach. He would act as if he didn't care about us, but would never give up on us just when we were getting going.

The guy got out by City Hall. Maybe that's why he'd been cracking his knuckles so nervously. I stayed on until the Galleria. My plan hadn't been to go to Rich's—I hadn't had a plan—but I felt as if I needed to say something to Ben. I wanted to blame him for something. Rich looked up from his old guys at the counter. It was embarrassing how often I had been in the store recently. Ben was nowhere on the floor. The old guys stopped talking when I went up to the counter. They smelled like cigars. I said, Is Ben working?

Rich said, Oh, you know Benjamin? Nice guy.

I said, Is he here?

Rich said, Couldn't say, sweetheart. He got rid of his Saturdays a few weeks ago. I think he has his, what's it called, gardening business going on the weekends.

I said, Landscaping. I said, Thank you, and bought a pack of Trident.

It was one thing to lie to me, or Rich, but to my dad? Who might actually hurt his back spreading wood chips? I hoped he hadn't given Ben any money yet. I got to the bus stop just as the 15, which crossed the river and went

up Morrison, was pulling away. The stop was in front
of the central library and I sat on the steps to wait for
the next one. The steps were damp. My butt was getting
damp from sitting on them. The other people sitting
on the steps were, I guessed, homeless. Their shopping
carts lined the curb. Homeless people used the library
bathroom as if it were their bathroom, which was fine.
One of the younger guys in a thick, ripped flannel had a
skateboard that he pushed back and forth with his feet
while he sat. He might have been looking at me. Ben's
address was on the piece of paper in my pocket.

The bus took me across the river and I got out at 20th
and walked two blocks east. The sign above the entryway
said The Alderwood. These kinds of old apartment buildings were all over Southeast. A tree—an alder?—was stuck
in a muddy parking strip across the street. It provided
some cover. The phone book hadn't listed an apartment
number, and the face of The Alderwood told me nothing.
One window had bright blue curtains. Three windows had
plants on the sill. Ben was interested in plants. Ben's being interested in plants didn't mean he had any. A gray cat
poked its head out a second-story window. A gray-haired
woman walked out of the building, carrying a bicycle.
There had been a Plaid Pantry back where the bus had
let me off. Inside, my craving veered toward savory, then
sweet, from Fritos to a Heath bar to a Slurpee to nothing.

No one was on the pay phone outside. Erika said,
Where are you?

I said, Just a pay phone.

Erika asked if I wanted to come over and do home-
work. A car revved loud down Morrison. Erika said,
Where are you?

I said, Downtown. But I'm leaving soon. I'll call you
later. I said, Someone's waiting for the phone.

There was a bus in the distance that was probably
mine. There was no reason for me not to get on it. A huge
cemetery spread out on the other side of the street. Ben
might have walked home through the cemetery as if it
were just another park. I went back to the parking strip
across from The Alderwood. There were sixteen windows
on the face of the building. Each apartment could have
been identical, or different, from the others. My brother,
if he had stayed, or if he'd left and come back, might have
lived in one of those apartments. He and Ben might have
been neighbors who kept their doors unlocked. They
could move through the two apartments as if they were
one. A tan car, a Datsun, pulled up across the street.

Ben said, Julie! He was smoking a cigarette. He said,
What brings you to these parts?

The cigarette surprised me, though it shouldn't have.
I said, I thought you were working.

Ben laughed. He said, Right. Sorry I bailed on your
dad today.

I said, So you finished work already? He didn't sound
sorry.

Ben looked at me and squinted. He said, Julie, I can
tell you this, right? His voice had a scraped-out quality
to it, as if he'd just woken up. He said, The truth is, I

had a late night last night and I couldn't muster for the viburnum this morning. Between us?

He didn't sound guilty at all. He wasn't acting as if he suspected that I might rat him out. I said, My dad ended up moving that wheelbarrow himself.

Ben put out his cigarette. He said, If you came over here to give me a guilt trip, I think I'm going to need some Advil with it. Want to come in? He walked into the building and held the door open for me. He took out a key and opened a long, skinny mailbox, and he took out some letters and a magazine.

I said, Then where are you coming from? I didn't care if the question was a hammer against his hangover.

Ben laughed. He said, That's a good question. You're a good questioner. He opened a door on the second floor and scooped up the gray cat as it tried to run out. Ben said, This is Patty. The cat meowed. Ben said, She's a good questioner, too. He said, Shoes, if you don't mind, and kicked off his sneakers.

Ben's apartment was small and very neat. The kitchen linoleum and metal cabinets looked old-fashioned, the refrigerator like something that could be called an icebox. Ben took out a beer. He said, I'm not going to offer you one. He opened the beer and swallowed some pills with it. He said, What would you like? Tea, right?

I said, How about coffee?

Ben said, Right on. I could use some of that, too. He got out a small metal pot and spooned coffee grounds into it.

My raincoat and backpack were still on. My shoes were by the door. I said, I can go. I had just shown up. There was no reason for me to be there.

Ben said, No, stay for a few. I'd be vegging on the couch with Divorce Court if you weren't here.

Ben's kitchen chairs had puffy vinyl diner cushions on them. Patty jumped into my lap. Ben said, Cat person?

I said, I don't know. Patty pressed her head into my chest.

Ben said, She's a sweetheart. He leaned over and scratched under Patty's chin. He said, Except when she's not, right, girl?

Ben moved around the kitchen, sipping from his beer, scooping out cat food, taking out mugs and acting as if there were nobody else in the room. His refrigerator had fliers photocopied on fluorescent-colored paper. They looked as if they'd been made in five minutes with a glue stick and scissors. I said, What's the Anchor?

Ben brought the two mugs of coffee and a carton of milk and his beer over to the table. He took a sip of his coffee and held it in his mouth before he swallowed. He said, Why, have you heard of it?

It was as if he hadn't been listening. I said, I just asked you what it was. I would have expected him to listen, after making a point of inviting me in and asking me—telling me—to take my shoes off in his kitchen.

Ben put his elbows on the table and his chin on his hands and leaned in and looked right at me. He said,

Did I do something to make you angry? Your dad didn't sound mad on the phone.

Ben's hair was greasy and the skin under his eyes was grayish. He wasn't making it clear whether he was pissed at me for being mad or if he actually cared. The coffee was doing something to me. I said, The other day, did you tell my dad I was at swim practice?

Ben said, What other day? I don't think so. He said, Why? Do they not know? He said, I get it, it could be heavy to tell them.

My skin moved. My whole body was a heartbeat. Ben must have made the coffee some special hangover strength and not told me.

Ben said, You can feel free to talk to me about it. He said, Or not. No pressure.

My mug had a picture of a four-leaf clover on it and it said Shamrock Run 1987. Ben didn't strike me as a runner. But he could have been, who knew? I didn't know anything about him. I said, It doesn't matter. I'm going to quit.

Ben said, No way! I thought you were into it.

I said, I hate the coach. I said, He's really judgmental. I said, I think he puts extra pressure on me, because of Jordan.

It hadn't occurred to me until I said it. I said, It's not like everyone's trying to be in the Olympics.

Ben said, Of course.

I said, And my friend Alexis? She should totally be in Lane One. She's basically the best breaststroker on the team. I said, Girls' team. I took another sip of coffee. The cup wasn't halfway empty.

Ben said, That coach sounds like a douche bag.

I said, He is.

Ben was touching the bead on his necklace. I could tell he was thinking about what to tell me to do. I would listen. He knew something, I could tell, about swimming.

He said, Well, how much do you like to swim?

I said, What do you mean?

He said, If you really love it, you shouldn't let some asshole coach make you quit. Jordan's coach was an asshole. He said, Not that Jordan thought so.

It was that thing he did, the loose way he threw around information about my brother. As if he were referencing things I was automatically supposed to know about.

The coffee was acid in my stomach. Ben's hangover brew or whatever it was was making me dizzy. On the wall was a crazily blurred pink poster. I said, What's that poster?

Ben said, Oh my god. Have you not heard Loveless? My Bloody Valentine? Of course you haven't. Hold on. He went into the living room and fiddled with the stereo and a needle-dropping sound came on and then a thick swath of music. The singer sounded as if she were under layers of gauze, or maybe water, something thicker. It was impossible to tell if she was trapped or if she was there because she wanted to be.

Ben said, If you like it, I'll tape it for you. And the R.E.M., too. It'll be fun. He said, Oh my god, I was always trying to force my music on your brother.

Someone made a sound in the next apartment—a clanging pot. The Alderwood had thin walls. Ben must have driven the neighbors crazy with that choked-syrup music he played. The Alderwood was clearly a dump. I said, My brother wouldn't live here. My coffee had little specks of grounds floating in it. I said, That metal pot you use doesn't work very well. I said, I have to catch the bus. My jacket was still on. I said, That coffee was kind of strong. Three or four sips had turned me into a tin can rattling.

AT LUNCH THE day of the meet Erika showed me that she'd written 100 Back on the back of her hand. The night before she'd waited outside until the clouds cleared so she could wish on a star. I'd never known her to be so superstitious. She didn't need all those charms. She was the best backstroker in Lane Four. I'd watched her. It was as if all she had to do was lie down on her back in the water and there it was, off she went, never swerving, never crashing into the wall.

She handed me the pen. She said, Do you want to write down a race?

I pressed the ballpoint into the skin on the back of my hand. I had to press hard to get a faint line of blue. I said, I don't want to jinx it.

Erika said, Crap, you're right. She wet her thumb and wiped at the writing.

We massed on the sidewalk, before the last bell, waiting to get on the bus. Alexis and Melanie stood near the curb, tented together. If Alexis looked over at me and waved and offered me something, some meet-day treat, I would wish her good luck when I took it. Greg walked over and Alexis put her arm around him and leaned against his shoulder, and he patted her head like there, there. The pat didn't strike me as sincere. Coach stood at the entrance to the bus, clipboard in hand. Erika was so amped up that I let her get on ahead of me. Coach said, Erika, nice job with backstroke lately. He told her she'd swim the 100 Back and the 400 Free Relay. She high-fived the palm Coach offered. When I stepped up Coach angled his clipboard toward him and looked down at it. He said, Julie. Glad to see you. He kept looking at his clipboard. He said, We've got you in the 400 Free Relay. I said, Okay, waiting for more. He said, So you'll be with Erika on that one. He said, We'll try to work toward a solo event for next time, okay?

Because Erika had gotten on first, she sat in my window seat, forgetting or ignoring that I always got the window. I stood in the aisle until she saw me and slid over to let me in. Coach went down the rows, handing out swim team sweatshirts to the people who had ordered them. They were expensive, and I hadn't wanted to ask my parents for the money. The bus was a heap of enthusiasm. People were waving their races in the air like flags, and nobody had won anything yet.

The meet was at Madison, they had their own pool, and the locker room was as clean as a hotel bathroom.

The locker room buzzed. Girls were talking to girls they would never talk to. I changed quickly and went into the bathroom stall for a pube check. My new green-and-white competition suit was tighter and higher-cut than my regular suit. There were two pubes showing below the leg-line—a pain at the pulling, then a pop. I put them in the toilet and flushed. Alexis was at the sink pushing stray hairs into her bathing cap. I hadn't thought before about how it would be harder for her to sweep her hair easily into a ponytail and cover it with a cap now that she'd gotten it cut. I saw her see me in the mirror.

She said, Oh my god, Julie, I'm so nervous.

I said, You're going to do great. I meant it. It was hard not to look at the reflection of her and me in the mirror.

Alexis said, Hey Julie, can I ask you a weird question?

I said, Okay.

She said, Did your brother do anything before a race? For luck or something?

I wished I had something to give her, for luck. A clover or a disc on a chain. I said, Let me think for a second.

I'd read a spread in the latest Poolside about swimmers' pre-meet rituals. Their answers had been pretty predictable—playing the Rocky song, calling their mothers. There was one I had liked. It had struck me as something my brother might do. I said, He went to sleep super early the night before, so he could get up and watch the sunrise.

Alexis said, That's sweet. She said, That's kind of romantic. But I missed the sunrise.

She was nervous, I could tell. I wanted to give her something else. I wanted it to be something she could use. I looked in the mirror and saw her nervous eyes blinking, her hands tapping against her crossed arms. I said, He also did a thing where he closed his eyes and breathed. Alexis nodded, and her tapping slowed. I said, Then he counted back slowly from ten.

Alexis said, Cool! She finished adjusting her cap. She said, That sounds easy.

THE MADISON POOL was cleaner and bigger than the pool at the Y. It may have just looked bigger because it was cleaner.

The Madison swimmers wore navy and gold.

The striver asked me if I was nervous.

The whistle the referee blew to start the meet wasn't louder or different-sounding from a regular whistle. I'd thought he would use the starting gun.

Alexis swam the breaststroke leg of the Medley Relay. Coach was standing in front of me, blocking my view.

We were allowed to have our towels on the pool deck. I wrapped mine around my waist.

The referee blew the whistle. A Madison swimmer had dived in too soon.

The Madison swimmers were bigger than our swimmers. They looked stronger. Their coach probably cut people from the team.

Erika told me to wish her luck.

Erika came in fourth, beating out Madison's B and C teams. PT came up and gave her a high five. When had she learned to do flip turns?

Someone tried to start We Will Rock You.

Someone tried to start a wave.

Coach, red-faced, yelled, Pull! Pull! He lunged close to the edge of the pool.

Alexis stepped up on the block for the 100 Breast. She swam stiff and stilted for the first length. I thought, I believe you can do this. I thought, Count back from ten. Midway through the second length, her stroke untensed. She smoothed the water. She took up and folded it. She touched the wall and the stands went crazy.

The striver asked me if I knew how many points were needed for a varsity letter. She was wearing a gray swimming sweatshirt. It swam on her.

I tensed for the crack and the starting gun went.

The 400 Free Relay was the last event of the meet. I had almost forgotten I had a race to swim. The C team was Erika and Donna and the striver and me. The striver tried to lead us in a cheer.

The gun popped. The striver dove. With her careful scoopings, she kept fairly apace. Donna, next, swam strong and sharp and pulled us a fraction ahead of Madison's C team. I climbed up on the block. I hadn't thought, all meet, about swimming. No one had mentioned how much the block slanted forward. No one had told me how to curl my toes or when to put up my arms for the dive. Donna touched the wall. I put up my arms and went. My body hit cold water. For a second I flailed, or my mind did. Then my arm went, then my other one, my legs did what they did and I got on the rails. I kept even and clean. I stroked and kicked and turned my head in rhythm. I came up on the wall and I touched, and turned, and I stayed on it, a good machine back down the lane. I counted backward from ten. I touched the wall, done.

Someone was yelling my name. More than one person. Donna was saying, Holy shit, she's stopping, and Coach was saying, Julie, keep going! I'd only done two lengths. I had somehow forgotten that I was supposed to do four. I arced around and pushed off with no momentum. I'd known 100 was there, back, there, back, but I'd forgotten, or I'd thought I'd done it all, or I hadn't been thinking, which was supposed to be the point. I chopped. I spat. My brain went everywhere, nowhere good. My suit chafed and rode up. It wasn't made for someone who was built like me. I slapped and churned. Finally finally finally the wall. Erika dove in. The A and B teams were finished, and the Madison C team, almost. Erika would be the last one in the pool because of me. My arms were spent. They used the last they had to hoist me up and out of the pool. I didn't say a word to Donna or the striver. I stood against the wall with my hands in fists. The striver said, It's okay, you forgot. If she offered me a tip, I would lose it. I was this close to losing it. The meet was over. Erika got out of the pool.

I said, I'm sorry.

Erika hopped on one foot, shaking water from her ear. She said, It's completely okay. Don't worry about it.

I said, I'm really sorry. I really fucked up. I wanted her to slice me with an accusation.

Coach came over. He said, Hey Julie, what happened in there, forgot we were doing a 100?

Erika said, It's my fault, we were talking about doing 50s right before she got in.

I said, I'm really sorry. Now I was completely crying. There was no way Coach couldn't tell.

He patted my shoulder. He said, You know what, Julie? It happens. It happens once so it won't happen again, right?

Erika said, Absolutely.

COACH STEPPED ONTO the bus and the team went wild. He put his hands up for silence. He said, Let me tell you what. We just beat the number one-ranked team in our division. And we beat them with some kick-ass races. Greg cupped his hands and said Alexis's name in a low, loud growl, and the back of the bus cheered and the cheer carried up in waves. I felt the waves pass over and around me. Melanie said, Party at Alexis's, and the cheers swelled again.

Erika said, Yeah, should we go? They were talking about it in the stands.

I said, I don't think I was invited.

Erika said, The whole team is invited. Let's go?

I let Erika convince me to come over to her house for dinner, where we ate mushy veggie burgers and Erika did most of the talking, describing how mean and ripped the Madison team was, and how she'd beat her best time on backstroke. She hadn't mentioned that she'd been timing herself. Erika's mom asked how it went for me. Erika said, Julie did great.

Erika's mom looked younger than my mom, not in her face or skin but in how she moved and talked to us. I said, She's just saying that.

Erika said, It was an honest mistake.

I said, I ruined the race. The veggie burgers were a lukewarm paste. I took another bite. I said, I'm thinking about quitting.

Erika's mom said, I don't think an honest mistake feels any better than a dishonest one. She put her hand on top of my hand and squeezed it. She said, I'm really sorry, Julie.

I didn't know what she was sorry about. I could have stayed in that kitchen for the rest of the night.

I lay on Erika's bed and looked away while she changed. I looked back each time she had something new to show me—two tight T-shirts that were the same except for their color, and a purplish button-down with the top buttons open. Erika said, Too slutty?

I said, Not if you don't mind Grapestuff staring at your chest.

Erika said, Really? Gross. She said, The question is how to get PT to look at my chest.

I said, Right.

Erika said, Stop looking at the ceiling and tell me if you think I should do two buttons or three.

I turned on my side to face Erika. I lay on my side while she said, Okay, here's two, and gave a little curtsy sort of flap of her hands at her sides. My eyes had nowhere appropriate to go. She said, Okay, here's three, and revealed the tops of her boobs—tits was the word I felt I should use—and the line of cleavage. I dipped my eyes there. It was what she was asking me to do—to put aside my, in her words, gloom and doom, and look at her as if I were PT. I looked full-on at Erika with her shirt half-unbuttoned, her tits hanging out, her bra almost showing, and a hum or a pulse hit my crotch area—my crotch or PT's. I sat up. I said, Start with two.

Erika said, You're right. PT seems like he'd prefer a little mystery. She said, You're not really quitting, right?

Erika said that if I wasn't going to borrow a shirt from her I could at least not hide in my hoodie, so I took off my hoodie and wore my second layer, my teal heathered henley, one of my favorites which, big laugh, I had put on that day for good luck. Erika said at least I could try wearing my hair down. I undid my low ponytail and put my rubber band around my wrist. Sometimes I forgot how long my hair was. My hair undone made my face too soft. It looked as if I were trying to look like something. I pulled my hair back.

GRAPESTUFF OPENED ALEXIS'S front door. He said, Ladies!

Erika said, What are you, the official door opener?

He said, Alexis's parents are at the coast. Keg's in the kitchen, ladies.

Alexis's house was full of swimmers holding big red cups of beer. The Beastie Boys blasted loud from the stereo. People raised their cups and yelled the words. It was a winners' party. I said to Erika, I think I might go.

She said, Stay an hour with me. Please? She said, There he is. PT was sitting on the arm of a couch talking to a butterflier. They both had beer. Erika said, Let's get some.

Greg was standing at the keg. He said, Step right up. He filled my cup and said, Julie, right? It's nice to meet you. It was a stupid thing to say, we weren't meeting now, and we had basically met before. And to say, now, that it was nice to meet me meant he was thinking about my ruined race and lying through his teeth.

I stood silently next to Erika while she talked to Lane Four swimmers and newspaper kids, a few groups over from where PT sat. My beer tasted like pee, or Swiss cheese. I took another sip. I didn't feel anything. I wanted the drinking to make me even less there. Every once in a while someone would cup his or her hands and say JACK-SON. And then cheering, even from the non-swimmers. Everyone wanted to be celebrating something, still, though the races were done and the points awarded. Winning dragged and dragged on. I said, It's probably been an hour. I can go by myself. Erika asked me how I would get home. I said I could call my parents, but the idea of calling them felt terrible, the idea of being in the front seat with my dad, with the radio playing and nobody talking, of getting home and being alone in my room.

I drank more. I had to pee. There was a long line at the downstairs bathroom. Someone said there was another one upstairs. I didn't care about waiting, I didn't have anything better to do, but I left the line and went upstairs to see more of Alexis's house. It was pretty fancy—up in the hills, the back held up by stilts. A big window at the top of the stairs had a view of the river and the lights and bridges. It was relaxing to look out at a view like that. The window was big enough that I could step out into it and be another shadow in the dark. Another cheer roiled up from downstairs. The worst was remembering the moment when I'd thought I was done—when I'd come to a stop I'd thought I'd earned. The view out the window was clear enough that I could step out into it and be as small and useless as a shadow, or the light's reflection on the water. A door down the hall closed and Alexis was standing next to me. She said, I love this view. She had on a light blue sweater.

I said, Congratulations.

She said, Thanks. I know. I was honestly surprised.

She was glowing so hard that there was almost room in the glow for me. Her sweater looked very soft. It was only a matter of time before she remembered what I'd done.

I said, I'm really sorry I messed up. My stare leveled out the window to keep me from crying.

She said, What? What happened?

It was nice of her to pretend she didn't know. I said, I made my relay team lose. The team lost those points because of me.

She said, Oh, whatever. What looked like a boat passed far away on the river. She said, Those points were nothing. No one will remember. The boat was a light tracking across our view. The smell of Alexis's conditioner curled toward me. The smell was a forest on a blanket in the sun, the smell from the hair of someone on the blanket beside me. Alexis leaned the weight of her left arm against my right. She tugged my cuff and said, Come here.

Alexis closed the door of her bedroom. She didn't turn the light on. She asked, Do you smoke? There was a pot pipe on her desk.

I said, No thanks.

Alexis came over and stood in front of me. She was around my height, an inch or so shorter. She took her hands and put them on either side of my neck, and slid her hands out to the ends of my shoulders, measuring me. She said, You have a really nice body, Julie. If I had been able to move myself away from her I might have. Alexis tightened her grip on my shoulders. She pulled me closer or pushed herself closer. The first kiss felt like a test. Her lips were dry and they pushed against mine and my air was gone, and then I felt her tongue. It was a soft, wet thing invading my mouth and my lips and my tongue did nothing back. She said, Is this okay? My mouth was beer-sour. It wasn't that it wasn't okay. I must have nodded, I must have made myself nod, because she came back and kissed me again and I was ready for it. I knew how to kiss her back. I pulled her lips with my lips and let my tongue touch the ridges of her teeth and her tongue. My hands touched her waist, and her sweater was as soft, softer, than it had looked, and it was easy to touch her waist and her hips and to press my hand in the crook of her hips. She took my hand and moved it up to her breast and pressed it there and took her hand away and I felt the weight and the heat and the outline of her bra underneath the thin sweater. Her nipple, as I touched it, got harder and she kissed me harder and my crotch pounded and her hips pressed against my hips. Alexis stepped back. My hair was loose, she must have unloosed it, and she combed her fingers loosely through it. She said, You're a good kisser. We were standing in the middle of her dark room. She said, Do you mind? and went and picked up the pot pipe and lit it. The pot glowed. She blew the smoke out in my direction, on purpose, a tease. I had to say something.

I said, I'm quitting the team.

She said, Relays are stupid. Relays are too much pressure on everybody. She stepped back over and put her hand on my shoulder. She said, You need to find your own race that you can really work on, that you can really make your own, you know?

She talked as if she had a plan for me. I was waiting for her to kiss me again.

She said, What about the 500 Free? That's a really good event. People give all the attention to the sprinters, but distance can be kind of, I don't know, magical. She said, Can you do distance?

I said, I don't know.

Alexis said, Your brother's time on the 500 Free was incredible. I saw the plaque. I think it might be really awesome. I could count laps for you.

She had me cupped, convinced. With her hand on my shoulder, she could have said anything.

Alexis took a step back. She pulled her fingers through her hair and straightened her sweater. She said, All right. She said, I'm going to go out first, if that's okay? Just wait a few minutes. She kissed me quickly, half on my mouth, and left.

When I got downstairs, the mood had shifted, or I had. I was less outside of the frenzy and more, not of it, but as if I were the air or the dust in the air, around and amid what was happening. Erika was standing in a group with PT and a few gothish girls, on the edge of the room, and she pulled me over. They smelled like cloves. Erika said, Julie! She said, We were talking about music. Erika was drinking her beer, or drinking another one. Erika knew less about music than I did. She mostly knew her mom's old records, Joni Mitchell, who she loved to say she couldn't listen to without crying.

One of the girls said, We were basically obsessing about My Bloody Valentine. If you know them.

I said, Oh I know them. In my dust-state, I felt generous. I wanted to give Erika anything I could.

The girl said, You know them?

I said, Loveless. I love that album.

They talked and I hazed and half-listened, saying things for Erika when she didn't have anything to say. PT seemed quiet and nice enough, hanging out behind his glasses and wool cap, the person in the group least trying to do anything. I got glimpses of Alexis in different parts of the room. With Greg by the stereo, with Melanie by the sliding-glass door, with a beer in her hand, getting louder. A hand light-touched the inside of my elbow and by the time I turned to look Alexis was dancing with Greg by the sliding-glass door, the lights of the river and the city beyond them.

A little before midnight, Erika and I were standing outside, waiting for Erika's mom to pick us up. Alexis had called from across the room, Julie, are you leaving? and she had raised her hand to wave goodbye, along with Melanie and Greg. She was drunk and ensconced with her friends, it was fine, and it wasn't as if I was thinking about whether what had happened would happen again, or as if that was all I was thinking about. Erika said, I think I'm a little drunk. Are you?

I said, A little, not feeling drunk, but generous.

Erika said, I can't believe how cute PT is.

I said, He seems really nice.

She said, We went outside and smoked cloves.

I said, That's great.

Erika put her head back and opened her arms wide, a cartoon of a drunk person high on life. She said, The air feels so good. She said, Do you think he seemed like he liked me?

I HADN'T PLANNED on kissing Alexis. To think that I might have, without realizing, planned for or expected it made me cave with embarrassment. To think that I might have made Alexis think I wanted to kiss her by the color of the shirt I'd worn or the spot by the window where I'd chosen to stand. That I might have made her think that I wanted her to kiss me.

I knew I wouldn't tell Erika, or anyone. Not because Alexis was a girl, or because I was—Alexis had a boyfriend, and had had other boyfriends before. I hadn't, so what, I would. I wouldn't tell anyone because no one who wasn't me could know what it had felt like to be standing in Alexis's room and have her step close, then closer. No one could understand that what it had been about was something so specific, the light blue of her sweater, the heat of her breast in my hand.

I lay on my bed, hands off myself, feeling, more than feeling.

COACH SAID, JULIE-JULIE! Thanks for coming down. He was sitting at his desk, eating a sandwich and looking at the newspaper. A brass instrument in the practice room next door struggled up a scale. Coach said, This sandwich! Between us, the bread's a little dry.

Coach's clippings were up on the wall. His Beavers medal hung from his desk lamp. Coach may have wanted to check in that I was okay after what had happened at the meet. I was okay. I hadn't been thinking about it. Like Alexis said, no one cared about relays. Coach's desk was empty except for the paper and his clipboard and a half-empty frame of hanging folders. It wasn't clear why he needed an office, or how being a swim coach was a full-time job. I sat down.

Coach said, I thought you and I could use a check-in. Is there anything you'd like to talk to me about?

The thick green paint on the walls looked like the kind that had lead in it. The air in the office was probably unsafe to breathe. I said, I don't think so.

Coach said, It seemed like you were a little p.o.'ed about that swimming pamphlet.

I said, I wasn't. I said, It doesn't matter.

Coach leaned forward and put his chin on his tented fists. He said, Because if you've got some beef with me, we can talk it out. He gave a little shrug. He said, But what I hate is to see you taking it out on the team.

I didn't know what he was talking about.

Coach said, I mean, I get it. No one's that excited about swimming the third leg in a relay.

Maybe Coach took my silence as agreement, or as a blank space he could keep flinging words at.

He said, But when you've got your team counting on you, you can't just stop in the middle of a race. That's moving into some moral territory, Julie. He took a bite of his sandwich.

From the hallway a cymbal crashed, or fell.

I said, I'm quitting.

Coach put his sandwich down. He said, Really? He said, Damn.

I said, I don't think swimming's for me. I picked up my backpack and put it on my lap. I waited for the feeling of a chain unclipping from a longer chain.

Coach said, Shoot, Julie. That's not what I was trying to say.

I said, I was going to come down here and tell you anyway. I unzipped and zipped the pocket on my backpack. I waited for the feeling of a free spooling out. Coach wasn't saying anything. I said, It doesn't matter.

Coach said, It matters to me. He tossed his sandwich wrapper and crumbs scattered on the desk. He said, Listen. You're not interested in that pamphlet? Toss it.

I said, I already did.

Coach said, Why don't you tell me your side of what happened in the relay?

I should have had my backpack on my back and been out the door. I should have been looking forward to three o'clock that afternoon when I'd stand by the school doors watching the bus pull away, seeing if

I could see Alexis through the windows, wondering if she'd miss me.

I took a deep breath in. I said, What would you think about me swimming the 500 Free?

Coach said, Excuse me?

I said, I might not quit. I said, Maybe I just need a race to make my own.

Coach nodded. He said, I hear you. Relays are key, but I get that. You want a little ownership.

I said, I know, sprinters get all the attention. But I think distance can be kind of magical.

Coach said, That's a nice way of putting it, Julie. I hear you. He pulled his ear. He said, I'm just not quite sure I've seen you loving distance.

I said, You mean the stopping?

A few days before the meet, I had come to the end of a length to find Donna standing in the shallow end, arms folded. She'd said, I'm just resting. She'd said, Ask Coach. I hadn't said anything. I'd turned around and kept going, though I had been planning to take a minute or two to savor the wall.

I sat up straighter. I said, I think it might have something to do with the people in my lane. Coach hmmed. I said, So what about Lane Six?

Coach said, What about it?

I said, You could let me swim in Lane Six, and I could train for the 500 Free.

It was an amazing idea. Coach chewed his lower lip. He tapped a pen against the desk. He said, It's a bit unusual. What about all your teammates who don't get their own lane?

I said, No one wants Lane Six.

He said, That's true. It's not great for morale. He squinted. I knew it was an act. He'd known how perfect the plan was the moment I mentioned it. He said, Okay. Okay, why not? Let's try it. Maybe distance is where you'll hit your stride.

AT THE BEGINNING of practice, Coach called me over and huddled me up with the top distance swimmers. He asked them to give me some pointers. They all said, Pacing. They said, Long strokes. The gangly pro who'd asked me about my brother at Grapestuff's party had won the 500 at the Madison meet. He said, Don't kick. He said, I kick, like, five times when I do the 500. It's a waste of energy.

Coach said, He's exaggerating.

The pro looked at me. His eyes were pinkish, from pot or chlorine. He said, Don't kick. Unless you're really a kicker. It's not worth it.

The distance swimmers went off to their lanes and Coach walked me over to Lane Six. I could feel the swimmers in my old lane watching me. I felt as if Coach were my handler, or bodyguard. I felt famous. Coach had me jump in and swim a few laps while he watched.

I pushed off. Nothing but a lane line separated me from the poolful of swimmers, but Lane Six was quiet. I couldn't feel any difference between my body and the water. I swam a smooth line. I was in my own pool. I was swimming the blue parts on a map of the world. I didn't try to swim fast, I listened to the water, I didn't kick, and it was true, Coach was wrong, in Lane Six I could swim 500 yards. I touched the wall and turned and kept swimming. My mind went to Alexis, not to her, but to the feeling of her, the change that had arced the air when she leaned against me and said, Come here. Lane Six put that feeling on my skin.

I pulled up to the wall to find out what Coach had noticed. He said, Okay, looks pretty good.

I waited for him to say something else. I thought he would say something about how well-suited he now saw I was for the 500, or he'd give me the one final key I needed to make the 500 work. I said, Do you think I should be kicking more?

Coach said, It looked pretty good to me, Julie. He blew his whistle and called out the drill to the rest of the team. He said, You've got the basic form down. It's just going to be a matter of getting over that psychological hump. The 500 can feel long.

It was true, I'd blown off his advice before. Now I was ready for it and he wasn't giving me anything. I said, Do you think I'm holding up my head too high? I said, Sometimes it feels hard to know how high I should be holding it.

Coach said, Sure, that's normal. He said, I'll check back with you in a bit. Why don't you do 200 pull and 200 kick, and we'll go from there.

Donna and the striver were standing on the other side of the lane line, listening. When Coach walked away, Donna said, Why are you in Lane Six?

I said, I'm in training.

Donna said, For what?

I said, 500 Free.

The striver said, Really?

I said, What.

The striver said, You get tired after four laps.

Donna said, If that.

The striver said, You stopped in the middle of our race.

I said, That wasn't why I stopped. Lane Six coolly called me. It wanted me to get back to it. It wanted me to do the 200 pull, all arms, easy, and maybe the 200 kick, maybe 100 of it, if I decided to be a kicker.

Donna said, You know what? If you want to swim in that losers' lane, that's totally fine with me.

It was pathetic. It was ironic, those losers. They weren't the ones Coach said had potential, or whatever it was, they weren't the ones getting tips from the pros. They didn't know what it was like to be in Alexis's or anyone's room, to have anyone push an arm against theirs before taking them there. Coach blew his whistle. Donna said, Saved by the bell, but it could have been me who said it.

THE TABLECLOTH WAS uneven beneath the plates and food. I took the cloth's edge and pulled it toward me. On the bus ride home Erika had asked what I'd been doing swimming in Lane Six and when I told her about the 500 she'd asked me if I thought I could do it, backtracked and said of course I could do it but she was surprised that I wanted to. She'd been as bad as Coach, putting a concerned look on her face and making me explain myself instead of saying she was happy for me.

My dad asked how swimming was going.

I said, It's fine. I had nothing about swimming to say to my parents. What I wanted to know, I didn't want to hear about from them. They'd use the wrong words, or they wouldn't have been paying attention to the right things. They'd have forgotten the things I most wanted to know: how he stroked, when he breathed, if he did or didn't kick. They wouldn't know, he wouldn't have told them, if swimming the 500 felt like swimming forever.

My dad said, Have you had any meets yet?

My mom said, Not that you have to tell us about all your meets.

My dad said, Right. We'd only come if you wanted us to.

It was the middle of the night in Germany. The early early morning. If my brother were still in training, it was around the time he'd be getting up. I shook the salad dressing bottle until the oil and vinegar and the flecks of herbs combined.

I said, I'm thinking about swimming the 500 Free. I said, It's twenty lengths, in case you forgot. Ten times there and back. I said, A counter sits at the end of the lane with a number chart to help you keep track.

My mom said, I remember that chart.

I said, Do you remember anything else about it?

My mom said she remembered it seemed long. She said it was the event when people got up to use the bathroom. She said she thought my brother had only swum it once or twice, it wasn't one of his main races. She clearly didn't know, or care, that he had set the county record.

It had been four years since my parents told me my brother was taking a break from swimming. They hadn't said if break was the word he'd used or the one they'd chosen. It wasn't as if they'd be the first ones he'd tell if he started again.

I ate a few more bites and excused myself. I ran up the stairs to my room. I wanted to be in close reach of my phone so I could pick up right away if Alexis called. She would be so happy to hear my news.

ON SATURDAY I woke up and went to the window. Ben's car was parked outside and Ben was in the yard, lifting branches in the drizzle. I hadn't heard Pledge barking or the bell. I'd been sleeping heavily. I thought I'd been exhausting myself the first weeks of practice, but now that I wasn't stopping, or was stopping less, I fell into bed flattened out, depleted.

A note on the kitchen table said Ben might be in the yard. I zapped my Lipton and went out in my sweats and rain boots.

Ben said, Just up? Lucky you.

I said, Do you always work when it's raining?

Ben said, If I want to live here and I want to work, I guess I have to. He had on solid-looking hiking boots and a Gore-Tex raincoat. I didn't feel that bad for him. He said, How nice of you to bring me coffee.

I said, It's my tea. I said, Do you want some coffee? If he said yes I hoped there was some left in the pot my parents had made earlier. Nobody had ever shown me how to make coffee.

Ben said he'd come in for some when he finished the row he was working on. What he was doing to the yard looked okay—some smaller shrubs and some taller ones, a cross between random and arranged. It looked, not perfect, but better than it had before. He said, I hope no other landscapers see me doing this. This is a really weird time of year to be planting.

I set up in the kitchen with my Rice Chex and the A&E. There were shows in the TV listings I knew about just from reading them. Ben might think it was funny, or cool in a way, that I knew something about MacGyver without ever having seen it. Ben knocked on the sliding back door. He slid it open. He kicked off his wet boots and put the raincoat over a chair. He said, My jeans are a little muddy, do you think they'll care?

I said, I don't care. It was my house, too. I got up and poured Ben a cup of coffee from the coffeepot and brought it over to him.

He said, Oh thanks, I like it black.

I said, I can get you some milk if you want.

He said, No, for real. It's great. He reached in the inside pocket of his raincoat and handed me a tape. He said, For you. One side was My Bloody Valentine and the other was R.E.M.'s Murmur. He said, I put a few extra songs on the R.E.M. side.

The handwriting on the front of the case was scratchy ballpoint. It looked like a little kid's writing. I said, You know Country Feedback?

He said, Fuckin' A. Only good song on the album.

Somewhere in the house, in the attic, or basement, there could be a boxful of tapes that Ben had made for my brother and that my brother had left here. Or were tapes from Ben something he would have taken with him?

The coffee was steaming Ben's cheeks. He still had the outside on him. I took a slug of my tea and it was the bitter, tannic end, the tea bag in too long, my favorite part. I said, Do you ever talk to my brother?

Ben rolled his bead. I was sure that my brother had given it to him. Ben said, Not for a while.

I said, How long?

He said, Jeez. When did he go to Berlin? Three years ago? He called me once right when he got there.

I said, What did he say?

Ben pressed his lips together and raised his eyebrows. He said, I don't really remember. He might have blushed, or it might have been the steam and the cold. He said, And what I remember, I don't think he'd want me to repeat to you.

Something swarmed behind Ben's answer. I thought I could hit it from a different angle. I said, What did you do last night? Did you have a late night again?

Ben laughed. He said, Oh my god, you're priceless. Do you want to just ask me what you want to ask me?

I said, What do I want to ask you?

Ben said, First with the magazine, now this.

I said, What with the magazine? Do you have it?

Ben said, God, maybe somewhere. But how do you know about it? It's not like he sent you one.

It was true, I didn't know how we'd gotten it. I couldn't imagine my parents going out and buying it any more than I could imagine my brother sealing an envelope, writing our address, licking stamps. I said, Maybe his coach sent it?

Ben said, That guy. Oh my god, he would. Then he stopped, like a cartoon of a guy running into an invisible wall. He said, Julie. Tell me what magazine you're talking about.

I said, Swimmers' World. I'm not sure of the exact issue.

Ben laughed and his laughter swarmed away from me. He laughed like there was a third person at the table who was telling the most insane joke. People could laugh however they wanted, but it was rude. It was annoying. I had never mentioned the magazine out loud to anyone before. I said, What is so fucking funny?

Ben was still laughing. He said, I'm sorry. I think I remember the article you're talking about. But I don't have it, I'm sorry.

I said, What magazine are you talking about?

He said, Did you try the library? They keep back issues of everything.

I said, Of course.

I hadn't tried the library. I hadn't thought they'd keep something as specific as Swimmers' World. I thought they just had Newsweek and Time and Sports Illustrated. I said, What magazine are you talking about?

Ben touched the tips of his fingers together around his coffee cup, too carefully. I wasn't interested in his carefulness. He said, I just wish I could get a better sense of how much you know about your brother before I, how should I say it, broach certain terrain.

He sounded like a professor. He sounded like a fake-British imbecile. Pledge started barking and a car drove up. I sat for a moment staring at him, my jaw set around a quarry of swear words. My mom opened the door and called, Julie, groceries! Everything was twisted. I was sitting across my kitchen table from a person who could tell me everything, and he wasn't telling me anything. I said, You're confused, and got up to help my mom.

ERIKA HAD ASKED me on Friday if I wanted to do something on Saturday night and I'd hedged. I'd thought there was a chance that Alexis would call me and ask me to do something, or just call me to talk. On Thursday in Yearbook I had found a Reese's Peanut Butter Cup in my backpack and when I'd taken it out to unwrap it she'd caught my eye and given me a smile that slivered me.

On Saturday afternoon Erika called me, hysterical. She was talking even faster than usual. She said, You have to tell me you're free tonight.

It was almost five. I said, I'm free.

She said, Thank goodness. Can you meet me at eight? We're going to the movies with PT and his friends.

I said, He called you?

She said, No no, I went in for Saturday darkroom and one of his friends was there, that girl Larissa from the party, and I made myself ask her if he had a girlfriend and she said they were all going to the movies tonight and did I want to come.

I said, Does he have a girlfriend?

She said, No, I don't know. Larissa said he has something with some girl from St. Mary's, she said it's complicated, but you're coming with me, right?

It wasn't necessarily my idea of a good time to hang out with PT and those photography girls, or whatever kind of girls they were.

Erika said, There'll be a bunch of guys there. I bet one of them will be your type.

My first urge was to say that I didn't have a type. I said, I like tall guys. I pictured a guy that was my height or a little taller, and was skinny but strong. He didn't look like Ben and he didn't look like Alexis, who looked nothing like a guy. Alexis was somewhere outside of this conversation. The guy looked, so what, like a boy version of me. In my head I dared Erika to find me a guy like that, to see what would happen when he met me, how quickly we'd go at each other, how manically the sparks would fly.

As I was getting ready to go out I had some second thoughts. There was still a chance Alexis would call, and I wouldn't be home. But would that be the worst thing, for her to miss me? She might go out, instead, to the movies with her friends. There were often big packs of kids at the Galleria or the Tenplex on weekend nights. I couldn't exactly see our two groups mixing, but I could feel what it would feel like when Alexis saw me from across the huge theater lobby. I put on my teal heathered henley. I took my hair down.

The movie, it turned out, was at a tiny old theater in Northwest. We met the girls from the other night and PT and two other boys, a short one with green hair and a tall one in a striped shirt. Erika whispered to me that the striped shirt was tall. His shirt was nice. These people were all clearly friends, and it made no sense that we were there with them. The theater was minuscule and mostly a dump. It had an elaborately painted ceiling for people who bothered to look up. Larissa kept smiling at

Erika and giving her the thumbs-up behind PT's back.
She was being too obvious, but Erika thumbs-upped her
back every time. Larissa maneuvered it so Erika entered
the row just after PT, which meant that she sat next to
him and that every five minutes she grabbed my arm and
squeezed it in spastic excitement. She should have been
grabbing PT's arm. She should have been doing something to him or with him if she knew what she wanted.
The movie was a collection or festival of animation for
adults, and mostly so boring, and pointless, cartoons
were for kids and once you took out the kid part there
wasn't much left. There was one that was funny, though
it was hard to say why. A guy kept taking out a saw and
sawing at a table and the woman, his wife, kept saying,
Stop sawing, and he said, I'm not sawing, and kept sawing. Then there was a nuclear meltdown. The cartoons
went on and on. Some didn't have words. I tried to tune
out and imagine that Alexis was sitting next to me, but
Erika kept squeezing my arm and leaning over and whispering, and Alexis would never be at this dumpy theater,
where the chairs were from some time, the 1920s, before
people realized movie chairs needed to be comfortable.

After, we had to stand around outside while they all
smoked cloves. Erika smoked one. For some reason un-
known to me there was a long line for the next showing
edging the side of the building. Ben was in the line, part-
way down the block. He was with a couple other guys
who looked something like him and something like the
guys I was with. They had jean jackets—one of them

had the sheepskin-lined kind that looked so warm—and
their hair was sticking up as if it were supposed to stick
up that way. Ben was laughing and looking like he was
having a really great time. That morning he had laughed
like that, too loud, as if there was someone else in the
room who was in on the joke. Anyone would call it para-
noid, but it was possible that he and those guys were
laughing about the same thing that Ben had been laughing about earlier, cloaking me out with their laughter
again. I went to the other side of the huddle, upwind of
the clove smoke, so he wouldn't see me.

PT and Larissa and their friends were all going to
hang out at striped shirt's house. Erika wanted to go. She
whispered to me, Wasn't I right? Aaron is completely
your type.

He had a cute face and I did really like that shirt, and
maybe if I hadn't suddenly felt so tired, or tired of hanging out with these people who, clearly, were including us
just to be nice, I might have come. I said, You should go
if you want.

SUNDAY WAS UNUSUALLY clear and cold. It was unusual for
it to be clear when it was cold out. When I woke up I
had gone to look out the window, though I knew Ben
only came on Saturdays. It looked like he was done
with whatever he'd been doing. It was possible that he
wouldn't be coming back. Something about seeing him

last night, or how far or close I'd felt from him at the kitchen table yesterday, made me nervous to show up at the Alderwood without calling. The paper with his number was in my desk drawer.

Ben said, Hey, as if he were expecting someone.

I said, No, sorry. It's Julie.

He said, Hey Julie. How'd you like the animation?

I said, You saw me?

He said, I'll admit, I was a bit surprised that that was your crowd. Clove cigarettes! My goodness.

I said, They're not my crowd. I said, I wasn't smoking.

He said, Clearly I'm not one to talk.

Talking on the phone with Ben was easier than talking to him in the kitchen. If I hadn't had the feeling that we needed to have a conversation that called for more privacy than the extension in my room would allow, I might have tried to have it there. Ben said, It looks like a nice one out there. He suggested we go for a walk in Forest Park. He said he'd pick me up at the bottom of the hill in an hour. Neither of us had to say that he shouldn't pick me up at the house. As I walked down the hill the colors—the sky, the leaves, the shrubs—were crisp from the rain, their one chance all winter to show something off. I couldn't give a reason for how good I felt.

Ben drove to an entrance to the park I'd never gone in before, up off Skyline. There was a dirt pull-off where he parked the car, and a steepish path descending. He said, You wore good shoes, right? It'll be a little muddy. There were leaves and trees all above us that filtered the sun and cut it in shadows like paper cutouts. We walked awhile on wet leaves without saying anything. It didn't feel like we had to.

I said, You can smoke if you want to.

He said, Ha. I am an addict, but I'm not going to smoke in a forest. He said, So if those kids weren't your crew, who were they?

It was easy to talk to Ben in the forest. I said, My best friend has a crush on one of them.

Ben said, Which one? The cute one?

I said, The one with glasses.

Ben said, The cute one. Water dripped from the leaves above us. Ben was a few steps ahead of me and he stopped and blew air out from his mouth. He turned around. He said, Julie, I don't know if this matters, but I'm just going to tell you. Not because I think you have the wrong idea, but just to clear things up. We're friends, right?

I said, Right.

He said, And you probably know already, anyway.

I said, Okay.

He said, Okay you know?

This was cagey, ruthless Ben, the one who would laugh his head off with someone else who was in on the joke. I'd meant it when I agreed that we were friends. Now he was veering. I said, Stop making me feel like an idiot.

I braced myself for the laugh again. We were standing even with each other. He looked at me and gave a little smile, a real one, and said, I'm sorry. He said, It's weird to talk about at this point, but you're just a kid. He had his hands in his pockets. He said, You know I'm gay, right?

It was warm enough out that I was wearing a sweater and no coat. I found a pilled ball of wool on my sweater to pull at. I said, Okay. Once I started picking at my sweater, it was hard to stop. I thought of the guy with the lined jean jacket. I said, Was one of those guys you were with your boyfriend?

He said, From the movie? No, those are my pals. They're sweet.

I said, Are they gay? He said they were. We walked a little more. The air in Forest Park was extra sweet. The smell came from the trees, and it was fresh and clear, a smell that opened up the air. I said, Was my brother your boyfriend?

Ben said, No. Not really. We fooled around a little in high school, but no.

I said, So he's gay.

It was weird that we were still walking. This seemed like the kind of conversation we should be having sitting still, at a long wood table, or on a log overlooking the river. It also seemed like a conversation we could only have if we were walking.

Ben said, I kind of hate that I'm the one to tell you this. No I don't. Sure, yes. He is.

I said, He had a girlfriend in high school.

Ben said, So did we all.

I said, Why weren't you and he—boyfriends?

Ben said, Oh I don't know. Chemistry? He was into older guys.

I wanted to ask something else but I didn't want Ben to think I thought all gay people had AIDS. There were so many layers of wet leaves and pine needles under my feet. It was possible that half the forest had sunk below me. Rotted leaves so soft and we weren't sinking. I said, Older guys like his coach?

We had come to a log. We didn't sit on it, Ben just rested his foot on it. I put my foot up, too. Ben said, Ech. Yeah, like him. What a sleaze.

I had only the faintest memory of the compact man with very blond hair and a moustache. He had taken my brother with him to San Diego, because he was my brother's coach and he was moving there, and it made sense that my brother went with him to continue his training, but, if I can explain it, the feeling had always been there that the trip was more than an airplane ride. I said, So the coach was his boyfriend? It felt stupid, these minuscule, simple questions. For whatever reason I trusted Ben to answer them.

He said, I guess you could say that.

The sun was making so many good patterns. I loved how it hid us as much as how it shone on us. Ben sat on the log. He picked up a twig and rubbed it on a patch of moss on a knot of the log.

I said, Stop sawing.

Ben said, You stop sawing.

THE FIRST PHOTOS in the envelope were of my dad on the
business trip he'd taken to Scotland, shots of sheep
and men in kilts. My dad in a kilt, a glass in his hand
of what was probably scotch. We weren't Scottish. A
man with a clipboard pointing to a poster of a scotch
bottle. It made sense that my dad had forgotten these
photos. The oldness of the film had done something
to the color, a dusty reddening in the darker corners.
I flipped through faster. Me reading an Archie comic
on the beanbag chair. A fallen tree branch in the yard.
A long shot of a pool taken from far up in the stands,
and the next was of my brother: wet hair, on a podium,
gold around his neck. We had an identical photo in a
frame on the mantel downstairs. My mom must have
brought another camera and developed her film sooner.
My brother's coach or a hired photographer must have
taken it and sent us a copy. I went through the rest of
the photos. There were no more shots of the meet, just
the grainy dark shots I'd taken of the rubber bands on
my dad's desk, of my sneakers, untied. For a second
I thought I remembered that when Alexis had mock-
posed for her portrait in Yearbook, I'd actually lifted
the camera and pressed the shutter. The last photo
on the roll was of my painted pinecone. A bar of light
struck through the frame like a ghost.

My brother on the podium, smiling, eyes to the
crowd, didn't look gay or not gay. I wanted a shot of his
coach. I wanted to remember what he looked like. Was
he cute, or hot? I wanted to know if, the first time, a guy

came on to my brother or the other way around. Was it
Ben? Was it an older guy? How would he define fooling
around? Did having fooled around with Alexis make
me gay and, if so, did it make her gay, even though
she'd had boyfriends in high school? Maybe I should
have fooled around with a guy first. Or I needed to try
it with a guy in order to decide. The Berlin I imagined
had narrow streets and alleys and bridges. Twice my
brother had sent us postcards with a piece of the Berlin
Wall inside a plastic bubble. Was he right there when
the wall came down? Was it such a crazy party? Did he
get drunk, and were there gay guys there? Was there
AIDS in Germany? It wasn't that late, or early, where he
was but, I didn't have his number. I knew where to find
it, in the Rolodex by the phone downstairs, but I didn't
want to wake anyone up.

BEFORE WINTER BREAK the school went crazy with candygrams. Every morning a group of girls, cheerleaders, got
on the intercom and sang a song about candygrams to
the tune of Jingle Bells. Candygrams were a dollar. They
were a construction paper candy cane or snowman attached to a real candy cane and they could be signed or
anonymous. The candygrams song lodged and crackled
in my head all day. Last year Erika had sent me a candygram and also a boy from math class who I'd never
spoken to who wished me a Reeeeeally Happy Holiday

and drew a ballpoint Christmas tree and a menorah and a question mark. At lunch I started humming and Erika said, Thanks a lot.

I said, Are you going to send PT a candygram?

Erika said, No way. Does he seem like someone who'd be into candygrams? Erika had been acting slightly pissed since the night of the movies, when I'd gone home instead of going over to striped shirt's house. They'd all smoked pot, and Erika had gotten so stoned that she hadn't said anything for the whole night except for one conversation with PT about swimming. He'd told her he found swimming kind of spiritual. Erika had said she almost didn't want to tell me about their conversation because talking about it might make it less real.

I said, You don't have to send me one either. Alexis would have a desk overflowing with candygrams, from people who were and weren't her real friends. I wasn't going to send her one. I wasn't sending one to anybody. Still I knew, when the cheerleader dressed as an elf came into my homeroom and dropped a snowman on blue construction paper on my desk, with a candy cane tied on through a hole punch, that my candygram was from Alexis. It said, Happy holidays, Julie! and had a picture of a heart, and a comma, and Alexis. It wasn't what it said. It didn't say anything. But at some point she'd taken a marker and written my name, and paid someone a dollar, and passed someone the paper with my name on it. I crunched on my candy cane at lunch and Erika said, Who sent you one?

I said, Remember that kid from last year?

AT THE LAST practice before break Coach crouched on the pool deck and told me not to apply force to my stroke until my elbow was above my wrist. He said applying force sooner meant that I was pushing the water down instead of behind me. That made sense. It was the kind of advice I was looking for. It was the kind of advice I could imagine my brother's coach having crouched on the deck and given him. It was impossible to imagine how the story went from there—if after giving advice the coach leaned in and whispered to my brother to stay after practice, or if he didn't need to whisper, if there was nothing unusual about him asking my brother to stay after, and it was what happened when he stayed that changed things. Or it could have happened out of the pool, during one of the times my brother's coach drove him home, which was normal, practice went long. I pushed off and my arm reached and my fingertips touched the water and went under. Then my hand, my wrist and forearm, and it was hard to tell when my elbow was exactly over my wrist. The coach putting his hand on my brother's knee in the car. The coach running his hand over my brother's shoulder and telling him he had a nice body, and was it something my brother had been waiting for, with or without knowing it? Was his hand already unzipping his coach's fly? I didn't want to think about it. It wasn't something I should think about. I reached my left arm and kept track of the position of my elbow. When my forearm was perpendicular to the pool floor I pulled back. The pull felt more forceful. It shot me forward. I hoped Coach was watching.

I finished my entire cooldown, which kept me in the pool for a few minutes after the whistle. When I came to the wall there was nobody else left in the pool. No one was on the pool deck. I didn't know where Coach could be. I put my hands on the lip of the wall and pushed myself up. I hung there a second, my lower half underwater. My arms had gotten stronger. My arms looked strong, holding me up, half in and half out of the empty pool.

I grabbed my towel from my locker and ditched my cap and goggles. No one was in the shower room. I faced the wall and let the water soak me before peeling out of my suit. I opened my eyes to pump the soap dispenser. Alexis said, Hey Julie. She had come in and started the shower two down from mine. She was already naked. It wasn't as if I hadn't glimpsed her naked before. Everyone saw everyone. She said, I was sure I'd be the last one in here. I was running around trying to find Melanie a tampon. Good friend, right?

Nobody talked in the shower. I couldn't say anything. I couldn't look at her, whether I wanted to or not.

Alexis said, What have you got planned for break? She spoke as if we were just having a normal conversation somewhere. I faced the wall.

I said, Probably going to Seattle for a couple days. It was a stupid way to say it—we always spent four days over break in Seattle at my aunt and uncle's. I said, How about you? I was already rinsed. I was going to skip conditioner, and turn off the water and beeline for my towel as soon as I didn't feel her looking at me.

She said, I'm going to Hawaii, believe it or not. The smell of Agree bloomed up in the shower room. The smell took me over. I felt crazy. I turned and looked at Alexis. Her eyes were closed and she was rubbing conditioner into her hair. It felt crazy that my hand had touched her body, that my palm had felt, through the softest sweater, what it felt like to feel her nipples get hard. Alexis opened her eyes. She looked at me looking at her. All I could do was turn off the water, hope the soap was off me, and trip out to my towel to get covered.

ON CHRISTMAS EVE we drove up to Seattle to stay for a few days with my relatives. We did the same Seattle tourist things we always did, the Space Needle and Pike Place Market and a cold, wet walk along the lake. The trip was boring in a way I didn't mind. My cousin brought his girlfriend, now his fiancée, to meet us for Chinese food on Christmas. I had once visited him in his apartment in Seattle, which was something like Ben's, though my cousin's apartment had newer things and fewer of them. He did something with computers. It was hard to believe that he, Ben, and my brother were the same age. On the drive home I sat sleepy in the backseat, watching the highway. It was usually one of my favorite parts of the trip, the highway and the scenery and the open, lazy vacation feeling. Erika was going to spend the rest of break back and forth between all the parts of her family, and

Ben was in Arizona visiting his parents, and Alexis, believe it or not, was in Hawaii, which, though a US state, was very far away. It wasn't that I wished school would start back up. If I wanted to keep up with my training I could figure out a way to go to one of the city pools, or the JCC if we were still members. We were coming up on the space-age hump of the Tacoma Dome. My dad said it first, and my mom and I joined in: Tacoma Dome, Tacoma Dome, feeling the words round and dome-like in our mouths.

We were settled in the living room with a movie just started and the phone rang. I went to the kitchen to answer it.

My brother said, Holy cow. Is that Julie? He said, I'm calling for Christmas. For a happy Hanukkah!

In the background I heard music and voices yelling, or talking loudly. I said, What time is it there?

My brother said, What? He said, What's been going on with you? What are you, starting high school?

He'd called last at the end of the summer. I said, I'm a sophomore.

He said, Of course. That's great. I remember those times.

The phone was cordless. I went as far away from the living room as I could before the connection got staticky, about halfway up the stairs. There were so many things I had to ask him. I said, What do you remember? I heard what sounded like glass breaking, or a bottle clinking another bottle. I said, Where are you?

My brother said, Oh, just out at a friend's house. A little holiday party.

It was three days after Christmas, and the middle of the night in Germany.

I said, What friend?

My brother coughed, or laughed. It was a dry, mean sound. He said, Let's see, whose place is it. Karl's? Or Jan's?

The names sounded like made-up German names. For all any of us knew he could be in New York, or London, or on the other side of town. He could be in San Diego, one hand on his coach's dick. Ben could have been keeping any number of secrets from me. I sat down on the stairs. I said, When do you think you might come for a visit?

He said, Oh wow. It's pretty expensive to fly back to the States.

I said, I bet Mom and Dad would pay for it.

He said, Oh I get it. Did they put you up to asking?

I said, What? The conversation was swarming away from me. I knew the call was expensive. Any minute I'd lose him. I said, I know you have to go, but I just wanted to ask. I said, in a rush, I'm swimming, and I'm doing the 500 Free, and I was wondering if you could give me any special tips or tricks or anything.

There were a lot of voices in the background. They were speaking German, or English, it was impossible to tell. My brother said, Let's see. Pacing? He said, Honestly, I fucking hated that race. It was boring as hell. What did you do to get stuck with it?

From where I was sitting, halfway up the staircase, in the dark, I could see out the windows along the top of the front door. Rain in the streetlights. The yard, the careful landscaping becoming a swamp. This wasn't my brother's dime—it was Jan's, or Karl's. I could sit there silent as long as I wanted to.

My brother said, Probably a good idea to put the folks on now.

I stood up. I said, Okay. I said, I'm not serious about swimming, and went downstairs to tell my parents that my brother was on the phone.

I STILL DIDN'T love the Loveless side of the tape Ben had made me, though some of the songs were okay. The fifth song in had a ferris-wheel feel to it and the guy's and girl's voices singing together in an upbeat way but separated by layers of fuzz, close and distant at the same time. The R.E.M. songs on the other side were less polished than the R.E.M. songs I knew. They sounded held together by Scotch tape. They were prickly, and they dug a warm groove into the room. When Country Feedback came on I usually had to stop whatever I was doing, which wasn't much—teaching myself origami from a book my aunt had given me, sorting clothes for the Goodwill—and lie down on the carpet. I could have spent an hour lying there listening to him sing It's crazy what you could've had. That line was the feeling of wanting, or of wanting things that were slipping away. It wasn't as if I had lost anything. I understood after a day or two that my brother wasn't going to call me back—that he couldn't, really, without making my parents wonder why he was calling again. Or that he'd have to wait long enough that it wouldn't seem strange that he was calling again. The song made me want to have lost something so that I could want it back. Sometimes, lying there, my back molding its impression in the fibers of the wall-to-wall, I thought about Alexis. I let myself picture her in the shower with her eyes closed, knowing or not knowing that I was watching her, and I let the feeling of wanting flood me.

I also did stretches for swimming. On my pool-blue carpet I touched my toes and crossed one leg over the other and touched my toes again, and I pulled my quads and circled my arms and put one arm across my body, pulling at the elbow with the opposite arm. I put on my competition suit and lay on my bed with my front half hanging off it and worked on my stroke, keeping my elbow above my wrist, making sure my head was high but not too high. I took my mom's Jack LaLanne weights and curled them until I saw hard curves forming on my arms. I looked in the mirror to see if the hairs I could make out below the suit-line would be visible to anyone else, and I got dressed and took a walk to the grocery store for a bottle of Nair. I spread on the pink cream. I stood still in the bathroom while it burned through the hairs like a pesticide.

ALEXIS OFFERED ME macadamia nuts. Melanie offered me a Mexican lollipop. Erika told me that she had made a New Year's resolution to ask PT out. I got stuck behind her in the bus line while she stopped to ask him how his break was. He had, I overheard, just become an uncle. Erika couldn't get over it. She thought it made him seem so sensitive. I thought it made him seem old. I didn't think it seemed like a great idea for her to ask him out, if she didn't know that he was going to say yes, or if he might say yes without meaning it.

We got to the Y and got suited and Lane Six shimmered me a hello. It had missed me. I was in a lagoon in Hawaii. The water was clear and the air smelled like heady pink flowers and Alexis swam a few feet ahead. I went arm over arm and my lane opened up to me. It welcomed the weights I'd lifted and the stretches I'd done and the hairlessness of my legs from ankle to thigh. When I finished my warm-up Coach was crouched at the pool edge, waiting for me. I didn't want to stop and talk to him. I wanted to keep swimming.

Coach said, Listen, Julie. I thought about it some more over break, and I've decided it's not quite fair for you to have this lane all to yourself.

A twig snapped in my chest. I said, You told me I could swim here.

He said, I told you we could try it out. He didn't smile or shrug his shoulders. He was looking out at the end of the lane, away from me. He said, And I've done some more thinking, and I talked to some other folks about it, and I've come to the conclusion that it's not going to work out.

I said, Who did you talk to?

Coach said, I had some conversations with some other coaches.

I hated the idea of Coach standing around talking about me with other coaches at what, a Christmas party? A bar? I said, No one else wants to swim in Lane Six.

Coach said, Unfortunately, Julie, that's not what it comes down to.

I said, Okay then, I'll quit. I knew, I had some idea, that I sounded like a brat, a bad baby making threats to get her way. But it had worked before, and I didn't care—I wouldn't go back to Lane Five, with the swimmers who passed me and hated me. I couldn't stand the idea of going back there. I made a New Year's resolution. I said, What if you just let me stay here and keep training until the next meet?

Other swimmers were starting to mass at the walls. It was time for Coach to stand up and call out the next drill. He looked at me without looking at me. He looked at me and thought poor him, it was so hard to be a swim coach. The next meet was in a week. He said, We can do that.

I said, How good of a time would I have to get? but Coach was already standing up and blowing his whistle and walking away from me.

IT HAD BEEN forever, it felt like, since I'd been to Rich's. New issues of Swimmers' World and Swimming Monthly were out on the racks. Swimmers' World was thicker but Swimming Monthly had more useful information. I didn't flip through to look for pictures of my brother. I took the magazine and brought it to the register. If Rich had a line about how I was finally buying a magazine, I would say there was a particular breathing technique in this issue that I needed to study closely.

Rich said, $3.95, sweetheart.

On the bus ride home I tore out the subscription card and filled in my name. I hesitated at the address. Maybe Ben would let me use his. But it would be a pain to have to coordinate with him every time a new issue came out. I filled in my address. I couldn't believe it had taken me this long to realize it: the point of swimming was to get good. I'd make sure the card went out in the next day's mail.

AN ANNOUNCEMENT CAME over the intercom during Yearbook. It said, Attention, swim team members. It said that due to a water main issue at the practice facility, our practice for the afternoon had been canceled. We should meet in the weight room instead. Erika said, Sweet. I knew what she meant but I didn't feel it. I needed every practice I could get.

Melanie and Alexis had been arguing all period. They'd argued through the announcement. Alexis wanted to have the front pages of the yearbook be in black paper and have people sign in silver pen, and Melanie wanted regular light-colored paper. Ms. C. pointed out that many people didn't have silver pens and Alexis said a perk could be that everyone would get a silver pen with their yearbook. Melanie said perks weren't in the budget. The bell rang and Alexis grabbed her things and was out of the room before anyone. Silver pens were a cool idea.

I hated weight room. Whenever I tried to move beyond the least amount of weight on any of the machines, Coach came by and pegged the weight one lighter, as if he were trying to hold me back.

I stopped in front of the trophy case. Someone had gone into it and polished everything. The glass front and the trophies shone. Whoever had polished the trophies had shifted them around a little bit.

Alexis said, You must have a ton of trophies at home. I caught her reflection in the glass.

I said, We have a few. It felt okay to be honest with Alexis. I could see myself, at some point, telling her about the call from my brother. Not everything, but about the music and the clinking bottles that were loud enough for me to hear over the phone, and she and I could wonder together where my brother would keep his trophies in an environment like that. We could imagine a duffel in the closet where he kept them for safekeeping, on occasion unpacking them to set up on mantels, using them to explain the life he'd had before.

Alexis said, It must be cool to have those around.

I caught both of our reflections in the glass. We looked like we belonged there.

Alexis said, Don't you want to just blow off this weight room thing?

She drove me in her white Taurus, which was messier than it had been the last time. The last time it had seemed like a newish car. It was raining hard and Alexis kept her eyes on the road, on the curving streets. She didn't speak or turn on music. I said, You're a good driver.

She laughed and said, That's a sweet thing to say.

I didn't want to say something sweet. This was the first time we'd been alone since the party at her house, the shower didn't count, and I wanted to say whatever was going to make the ride not end at my house in two minutes. Because it was all I had, I tried to think of my brother, with his high school girlfriend, or boyfriend, whatever, an older guy. I turned to face Alexis as fully as I could and said, Let's go to your house. She slowed the car and pulled over. We were a block from my house. She had her hand on the gearshift. If I had been my brother, or Greg, or anyone else, even Erika, I would have been able to take my hand and put it over hers.

Alexis said, Okay. She said, Julie? She said, Never mind. She drove her car past my house and around the hill to hers. Within a few blocks her hand was on my thigh. Within minutes of getting inside her house and throwing our bags and shoes and coats in the front hallway, and her saying hello to a woman vacuuming downstairs, we were in her room and she'd locked the door.

It wasn't as dark in her room as it had been the night of the party. Weak light came in through the windows. I stood in the same place I'd stood the last time. I didn't know where else to stand, or what to do. Alexis clicked around a stack of CDs. What she put on sounded familiar, bluesy guitar and a smoky voiced singer who swallowed his words like Elvis. She said, Is Chris Isaak okay? I didn't care what music she played. Maybe the hand on my thigh had been an accident. Alexis took my hand and walked me over to her bed. She lay down. I lay down facing her. She pushed some hairs behind my ear. She said, I told myself I wasn't going to do this again. But you're so cute. She kissed me, and her mouth felt hungry and wet, too close. I wanted to be at home, by myself, with my memories of the first time she'd kissed me. That was a stupid thing to want. I was where I had angled to be. I kissed her back. She rolled on top of me and rubbed her knee into my crotch while she kissed me, and the feeling was so huge that I rolled her over and did the same thing. She moved with my knee. She moved as if I were making her move like that but I could tell that her moving controlled me. My hand touched the bare skin of her stomach and she said, Your hands feel nice, so I pushed my hand up under her shirt and felt her bra, which was silky and taut, and she pressed up into my hand and then she stopped kissing me. She sat up. I had done something wrong. She took off her shirt. She tugged on my henley and said, Take that off, and I took it off, and she said, That too, and I took off my T-shirt, and it had been cold out so I had a tank top on beneath my T-shirt and she said, So many layers, and then she smiled and said, I like it. She cupped my bicep and said, Nice muscles. She pulled the rubber band from my hair. She pulled me to her, my mouth to her neck, and I kissed her there and she made a low sound and I kissed her there again. She said, No hickeys, okay? I put my mouth on her shoulder, her ear, and she pressed her hand into my hair and said my name. It didn't sound like my name.

I kissed her neck again, lightly, and she got quieter. I thought that meant she was done. I thought she'd reached the point where she'd sit up and stop and go take a hit of pot and ask me to wait to walk out after her. She took my hand and put it low on her stomach and said, I want you to. Or maybe she said, I want you.

I said, It's okay.

She looked up at me. Her cheeks were pink. She said, You don't want to?

I was half holding myself up with my left hand, my right on Alexis's stomach, and I wanted to move my right hand, to stop holding myself up, but I couldn't. Was this what I had asked for? She was closer to me than she'd ever been, pink cheeks, thick breathing, hair messy on the pillowcase. I said, I do. I said, Do you?

She said, You're so modest, Julie. I unbuttoned her jeans and unzipped them. She was wearing silky underwear that matched her bra, and I saw the strip of white skin from her tan line. She'd gotten really tan. She took my hand and pressed it to the crotch of her underwear. It was warm and damp. I pressed in a rhythm and she moved against me. She said, Harder, and I pressed harder. The underwear was thin. My hand slipped and pushed the underwear aside and I said, Sorry, and she said, No, do it, and I put my hand inside her underwear and moved it until she said, There, and I did what she said, I touched her and touched her there, doing exactly what she told me to do, I kept touching her until she grabbed my wrist and said, Okay, okay.

I said, I'm sorry.

She said, Ssh. She said, Just press there for a minute. I felt her beat back against me.

The light from the windows was almost gone. I was lying half on top of Alexis. She rolled out from under me and looked away, a little shy, or fake-shy. She said, Whew. She said, What will we tell everyone when they ask why we weren't at weight room? She gave a big sigh and leaned up on her elbow and looked at me. She pushed my hair around. She said, You have a nice face. She touched my cheekbone. She said, In a way I think you don't look like your brother, and in a way I think you do.

Chris Isaak was singing Wicked Game. She said, I think this song is so sexy. And have you seen the video? She fell asleep with her hand on my chest.

PLEDGE LAY ON my feet at the foot of my bed. Light came in through the blinds and I didn't look to see what time it was. I'd thought that if I could make myself stay in bed until seven, then I could give up and get dressed and take the bus downtown to Mar-Shell's for breakfast. I wasn't hungry. My mind was awake and my body was too tired to move. My mind went and went to when I'd told Alexis to take me to her house. To when she'd put her hand on my thigh. I had to make myself think about the rest. My knee pushed at her crotch and my finger slipped inside her. I couldn't see myself doing those things to her. I made myself into a guy with a dick. My dick got hard and went inside her and I didn't have to think about anything. My dick pushed into her until she grabbed my wrist and said, Okay.

I wished Alexis were lying next to me. I wished that her hand was on my chest as if holding me there, saying, Stay. We had lain in her bed for who knows how long, an hour, while she napped and I buzzed and watched the light leave the room, listened to the CD finish and click over to the next one on the changer, and then the phone had rung. I'd touched her hair and said, The phone's ringing. She'd looked at me sleepy-eyed and smiled and rolled over to answer it. And her voice had changed after she'd said hello, and she'd sat up and put her shirt on, and she'd said to the person on the phone that she'd had a headache but it was better now, and she'd said, Seven? Okay, and hung up and smiled a little more tightly and said she should probably shower and stuff, and she hadn't offered to drive me home.

My fingers still smelled like Alexis. They smelled like sex—if what we had done was sex. What I had done to her. On the ride home with my dad I'd held my breath in stints because I had to believe that what I couldn't smell my dad couldn't either. I dozed and when I woke I turned on my clock radio. Two songs in, Wicked Game came on. It was as if I had asked for an omen. The phone rang, and I bolted up to answer it.

Erika said, Why weren't you in weight room?

I had had two messages from Erika when I got home from Alexis's. I said, I think I might be getting swimmer's shoulder. I pressed my thumb into my shoulder joint and felt an ache deep down.

Erika said, Why didn't you find me and tell me?

I said, I wasn't in the mood to go in front of everyone and talk to Coach about it. I said, Was he mad? Skipping weight room could have been a huge misstep. It could have been all he needed to change his mind for good about me and Lane Six.

Erika said, He didn't take attendance. There were a bunch of people who weren't there.

I pictured the dingy weight room, half full. If there were lots of people absent, nobody would have noticed that both Alexis and I weren't there. Nobody would have figured out that we were gone together.

Erika said, Well, I was worried. Then she told me that when I hadn't shown up she'd rallied her resolve and asked PT to be her spotting partner, and they had gone around and done the machines together, and how he was stronger than you might think, especially his legs. He'd said his friends made fun of him for being such a jock, and she loved that, how he was the least jocky jock and also that he would do what he wanted no matter what his friends thought. And he'd invited her to come see his friend's band play at Thee O tonight, and I would come with her, right?

I said, I don't think I can tonight.

Erika said, What are you doing?

I said, My parents want me to have dinner with them.

Erika said, The show doesn't start until ten. You can sleep over.

It felt wrong, and I knew that if I ever needed to see someone's friend's band play, Erika would go with me. Erika knew almost everything about me, except what she didn't know. I said, I'm actually going to see that guy.

Erika said, Which guy?

I said, That older guy I met. The landscaper. He called me and we're going to—I pulled for a plausible idea—we're going to go get coffee.

Erika said, At night?

I said, I'm meeting him when he gets off work.

Erika said, You were going to not tell me about this?

If half the team had skipped out on weight room, no one—not Erika or Greg, not Coach—would have thought Alexis, Julie, I wonder what they're doing? I said, I was just nervous. You know how sometimes when you tell someone about something it becomes less real?

Erika said, Well, you'd better tell me about it. She said, We're going to have a lot to talk about tomorrow.

**ON SUNDAY MORNING** I rang Ben's buzzer and in the silence after it I thought that he might be with a guy. The safe thing would have been to call first but I wanted the feeling of just stopping by. Ben came down the stairs in his socks, Patty the cat in his arms. I said, I was just stopping by. He was listening to loud guitar music, which he lowered, and he poured me a cup from the metal coffeepot. He said, Hungry? He said, Shoes?

I kicked mine off. There was a nice light-blue hoodie draped over a kitchen chair. I had no clue what kind of guy Ben would go out with. I said, Whose sweatshirt is that? Did somebody leave it here? I said, Is it a bad time?

Ben said, As it happens, it's mine. He put it on and zipped it up and unzipped it. He said, You like? He said, You're not catching me in the middle of something, if that's what you mean.

I said, I wasn't talking about that.

He said, But you could also call before you come. On a Sunday morning. Just to check in.

I said, I'm sorry. I can go.

He said, No, no. Just in the scheme of things. He picked up a metal mixing bowl and banged a fork around in it. He said, Stay. I'll make you eggs.

I let the coffee wet my lips. The same fliers were on the refrigerator. I said, Is the Anchor a gay bar?

Ben said, Yeah. Want to go?

I said, I'm fifteen. I said, I don't drink. I said, Why are you asking me?

Ben put his hands up above his head, palms out. He said, Joking, joking. He put a plate in front of me with scrambled eggs on it and a clump of soft, slimy grass. He said, You have to try it before I tell you what it is.

The greens tasted like dirt and butter, as if the butter were there to hide the dirt, but not entirely. I said, It tastes like butter.

He said, I know, that's the trick, right? He said, Wait for it. Sautéed spinach ends. He showed me a few left on the counter. At the bottom of the leaves of spinach, which apparently came in a bunch, were pinkish white bottoms.

I said, This is what you eat for breakfast?

He got his coffee and sat down with me. He said, I can't take credit. My friend Luke was the inventor.

I said, Was he your boyfriend?

Ben said, If only Luke had not been tragically in love with New York City, perhaps he would have been my boyfriend.

I said, But you—fooled around with him?

Ben took a sip of his coffee. He took another sip.

I said, You don't have to answer.

He said, No, look, I realize that I'm the one that opened this can of worms. Can of beans? Which is it?

I said, I don't know.

He said, What if I give you, like, five questions. Or five minutes?

I said, You'll answer them?

He said, I guess I'd have to.

I forked through the spinach ends. I said, So you'll be like the genie in the lamp.

He said, Allow me to be your genie for five minutes.

I said, Five questions. I had to make them matter. I hadn't come over to tell Ben about what had happened with me and Alexis, but he was the person I could most imagine telling about it. Anyone else would decide that they knew what it meant or didn't mean, that they had a name for it. I said, How did you know you were gay?

Ben said, That's your first question?

I said, Or when?

Ben said, Usually when people ask me that question, I like to turn it around and say How did you know you were straight?

I coughed, to cover whatever sound might have come out of me if I hadn't. I said, You're right, that was a stupid question. I looked at him as quickly as I could. I couldn't tell if he was laughing at me.

Ben said, Stupid questions still count.

I said, I know. I wanted to get away from that question as quickly as possible. I said, Do you have a boyfriend?

Ben said, Not currently. Next?

I said, I'm sorry.

He said, Don't be. He said, Next?

I was asking the questions but I felt as if Ben were leading the conversation. This was my chance to find out things I needed to know. It felt like a door he could see through but I couldn't. I said, What was the other magazine?

Ben said, What magazine? Then he said, Oh. Am I allowed to pass?

I said, No.

He said, You're right, that's not fair. This is just between us, right? He said, It was what I guess you'd call a porn mag.

I said, No.

Ben said, It wasn't super hardcore or anything. He just needed to make some money after the swimming thing ended and he split with his sugar daddy.

The spinach left silt on my teeth. It had seemed okay at first but it was actually disgusting. I said, A porno, like there were naked pictures of him in it?

Ben said, Is that your fourth question?

I said, No. I didn't need to know. I couldn't believe Ben had told me. My parents couldn't have known. They would have given him money.

Ben said, As far as I know, he only did it the once. It's not that big a deal.

He was lying, but I let him.

Ben took a big forkful of eggs. He said, I'll tell you one thing. Jordan would not have abided my spinach ends. He had the worst sweet tooth of anyone. He'd get those little mini boxes of Froot Loops and just throw them back. He said, But you knew that.

The loud record had ended. I put my lips to my coffee.

Ben said, Just so you know, it's okay that there are some grounds in there. It's Italian.

I said, What about the necklace my brother gave you?

Ben said, Which one?

I said, The one you always wear. The one you're wearing.

Ben said, This one? He ringed his fingers around the bead as if he were protecting it. He said, This isn't from Jordan. I got this necklace from my friend who died.

I didn't want to ask any more questions. I said, How did he die?

Ben said, He had AIDS.

A dark sewer surged up in me. It had been there and I'd pushed it down and now it came up so fast I thought it might black me out. I had to make myself ask before it flooded me. I said, Does my brother have AIDS?

Ben rubbed the bead the way I'd seen him do before. He was thinking of his friend. He said, I don't know. He could. He pushed on a smile. He said, But he probably doesn't. He was always really safe.

Blood transfusions, since Ryan White, were safe, and AIDS didn't come from toilet seats. We'd all seen the photos of the thin men with sores. I let Ben lie. My brother could have been calling from anywhere. He could have looked like anything.

Ben's face was a pale knot. He was loose-holding his necklace. Then I felt really sick, a sour mash of coffee and dirty spinach. I said, Do you?

Ben said, No. For now. He slapped his hand against the table, hard enough to make the plates jump. He said, Knock on a motherfucking slab of wood.

WHEN I GOT home I told my parents I wasn't feeling well and was going to lie down. I switched off the ringer on my extension. I lay on my back on my carpet. With my eyes closed or open I saw pictures of men with sores on their faces. Their hair was buzzed short and they wore dirty gray clothing that hung off their emaciated bodies, part AIDS, part Auschwitz. They leaned against tiled walls in dingy bathhouses. They wanted me to help them and I couldn't, or wouldn't. Their skin, if I touched it, would flake off in my fingers. I wanted a book with those pictures in it. I wanted to look at the pictures and keep myself from looking at them.

I went back down to the living room. I stood in the doorway. I said, Remember how Jordan was in that magazine, before the trials? I said, The swimming magazine. I pressed down my nausea. I'd never sounded more normal. I said, I was just wondering, do we have a copy of that magazine somewhere?

My mom said, It's probably in the file.

I said, What file?

My dad got up from the couch and I followed him down to his office. He moved some things around in the closet and pulled out a box made of cardboard patterned to look like wood. It had a wood-patterned top that lifted off, and in it were file folders, some with folded newspaper poking out the top. My dad reached in and came up with Swimmers' World, Summer 1987. It was pressed tight and thinner than I'd remembered.

I said, Did Jordan leave this box here? The closet had been his closet. Maybe he forgot the box, or left it with my parents for safekeeping.

My dad put his hand between my shoulder blades and patted me softly once, twice, as if I were a baby or a pet. He said, I don't think Jordan knows about this box.

I said, Is it okay for me to look through the whole thing?

In Swimmers' World, I looked first at the section with photos of swimmers in and out of the pool. My brother wasn't a big enough deal to be in that section. He was deeper into the magazine, one of ten Faces to Look Out For in the upcoming trials. Each of the faces had been asked the same questions. For favorite food, my brother said Caesar salad with extra croutons. For lucky charm he said some old dog tags his best friend had given him. I had no idea who that could be. His hometown was listed as San Diego, CA. They must have interviewed him in San Diego and forgotten to ask where he was really from. The photo showed him from the shoulders up. His shoulders were muscular and not particularly broad. His height was listed as 5'8". I was almost that tall. He had bleached blond hair growing out at the roots. He had a huge grin on his face, clear, healthy skin, and someone's hand clasped on his shoulder. His coach's? A guy from the team? I stared hard at the picture. I looked at my reflection in my dad's computer screen. In a way I looked like my brother, and in a way I didn't.

The other files in the box held newspaper clippings from state and county meets, the program from the big meet in San Diego. My parents and I had stayed in a fancy hotel suite on the water with a whirlpool bathtub and a basket of fruit and champagne. The grapes were as big as golf balls. The pool was so huge I couldn't keep track of my brother. It was an important meet, maybe the last one before the trials, and my brother had placed in all of his races. He'd stepped up onto a platform to get his medals and everyone in the stands, people who didn't know him, or who I didn't know knew him, were clapping for him. I remembered that there had been a plan to go out to dinner with us and the coach and my brother, but for some reason it hadn't happened.

In the back of the box were some small white envelopes that I thought for a second were letters from my brother—he'd been homesick, he missed us, he'd gotten sick of the sun. The envelopes held brief updates from his coach, form letters acknowledging receipt of funds. Did my parents know what was going on with him and my brother? Like me, did they know without really knowing? My dad's steps sounded on the ceiling above me. Behind all the papers was a tangle of medals. The satiny ribbons had pulled in places. These were the kinds of things we'd lay out at his funeral. We'd frame a copy of the Swimmers' World article and call the San

Diego line a typo, not tell anyone that his favorite food was really Froot Loops, he ate it by the bowlful, anything with sugar. I unknotted a small gold medal from the bunch. It showed a swimmer's arm angled out above re-liefed lines of water. Ben might want one. Alexis might want to see it. The cold disc warmed in my palm.

MELANIE OFFERED ME a granola bar. Alexis leaned her head on Greg's shoulder. I stood in the bus aisle waiting for Erika to let me in. She said, Are you sure you want to sit here?

I said, This is where we always sit. She moved her knees to the side as if I were a stranger in a movie theater.

She said, So did you not get my messages?

I said, I told you, I had a headache.

She said, What about when I called in the morning and you were out?

She'd already called twice when I got back from Ben's. I said, I was at the library.

She said, What about your swimmer's shoulder?

The more Erika came at me, the more I emptied out. It didn't matter what I said to her. I said, My shoulder's okay.

Erika said, Why do you have so many things wrong with you all of a sudden? She worked her eyes into a glare.

I said, I've been training harder. I don't know.

She wiped her eye with the cuff of her jacket. She said, I know you think my feelings for PT are stupid.

Her feelings weren't stupid, but she was obsessed with them. I would never say it, but Erika was nothing like the girls a guy like PT would like, and that made her feelings mean less. They had nothing real to catch on to. I said, I don't think your feelings are stupid. I said, How was the concert? I was going to ask you.

She said, Were you? Erika, even trying, couldn't sound mean. She said, Are you really asking me? She said, It was a show, not a concert. She said, PT didn't say that the friend in the band was his ex-girlfriend from St. Mary's. I basically had to spend the whole night watching him look at her.

I said, That sucks.

She said, It's not like they're back together, but the point is I don't do anything cool.

Alexis's laugh separated from the din at the back of the bus. I had thought, while I lay on my carpet, that if I found out my brother had AIDS and was dying, I would tell Alexis. She would be the one to tell, because in some way she felt something for him. We would be alone, in her room, and she'd tear up when I told her. We'd lie on her bed next to each other, and she would work her fingers loosely through my hair. We'd want to make out and know we shouldn't because the news was so sad.

Erika said, I was thinking. Maybe we should start a band? She said, Don't you have a guitar? I could sing.

My dad's old acoustic guitar sliced my fingers when I'd tried to play the chords he'd shown me. It was going to be hard for me and Alexis to find time alone together, with practice every day. I said, I'm pretty busy right now. I'm doing this whole training thing.

Erika said, Oh right. She wasn't mad anymore. She said, Maybe in the spring. She was so much more comfortable not being mad at me. She said, Really I just wanted to ask you about your date with the older guy. Tell me everything.

I used the side of my fist to clear fog from the window. If my brother had really been safe, Ben wouldn't have needed to say it. Ben knew, maybe better than anyone, that my brother was the type to go to a bathhouse and have sex with ten men whose names he didn't know.

I said, He canceled at the last minute.

Erika said, Oh no! She looked disappointed. She said, So disappointing. Did you reschedule?

With the last bit of generosity I could dig up, I said, Actually, it turns out he has a girlfriend. I said, It's okay, he was too old for me.

AT ONE POINT during practice, midway down the lane, I breathed to my left and I saw the striver on the other side of the lane line, swimming in the same direction, a few feet ahead of me. My head was where her knees were. I knew this was a test. It was as if someone had handed me a sword and said fight. My lungs worked. My arms sloughed off old water. My body pulled even with hers and we matched strokes with each other, scoop to kick and neck to neck.

We were stopped in time. We inhabited the same moment in time. We were insects in amber and the water pushed against us and then I pulled ahead of her.

I LAY IN bed and looked up Alexis's number in the phone book. I read her address and her last name. They hummed off the page at me. I turned on my back and brought the book to my face and smelled the cheap, slurry scent of newsprint. My fingers, for days, had smelled like Alexis, or they hadn't but I'd smelled her on them when I breathed in deeply enough. There was no one to tell me what was normal. My parents' footsteps sounded on the stairs and I pushed the phone book to the floor. It was late. I didn't have Alexis's private number. I'd forgotten to ask, or she'd forgotten to give it to me. I waited until I heard the TV murmur from my parents' room and I picked up the phone and listened to the deep, rich hole of the dial tone.

She'd say, Hi.

She'd say, I was just thinking about you.

Or she'd say, What's up?

I'd say, My brother's dying, and I'd wait for her to melt with sympathy.

Or I'd say, Not much.

She'd say, How's the training for the 500 Free going?

I'd say, Pretty good. I'm really building strength.

She'd say, That's great.

I'd say, How are you?

She'd say, I had kind of a crappy week. Or, I had kind of a shitty week.

I'd say, Why?

She'd say, Melanie and I keep arguing about this yearbook stuff. And Greg's not being helpful.

I would feel helpful. I would ask her to tell me what was going on. She'd tell me about the argument over the black paper.

I'd say, Silver pens are a cool idea.

She'd say, Thank you so much for understanding. That's so helpful. Then she'd say, I was just thinking about you.

MELANIE CAME OVER to our table with another stack of photos for us to ID. She said, So am I going to see you two at my house on Friday night?

Erika said, What's at your house Friday night?

Melanie said, I thought Alexis had invited you. She said, I'm having a big girls-only slumber party thing at my house after the meet.

Alexis came in and Melanie said, Al, I can't believe you didn't invite these girls to my thing on Friday.

Alexis said, Sorry, I've been so busy. She'd been back and forth to the copy room all period. She was busy with ads. She said, You're going to come?

Melanie said, We'll watch movies and do face masks. Have you ever seen Grease?

Erika said, We're free, right, Julie?

I didn't like Alexis standing there while Erika said we, as if Erika and I always did everything together, as if Erika were the master of my schedule. Alexis looked a little stressed, standing there with an armful of copies, but not flustered, or annoyed at Melanie for bringing up the party. She wasn't trying not to look at me. I had no reason to believe she'd been anything but busy. I said, not very loud, You want me to come?

Erika said, Duh, they just invited us!

Melanie gave us her address. After they'd left Erika said, Well, that was bizarre.

I said, What was bizarre about it?

Erika said, It's just weird to me that they like us. Or act like they do.

I said, What's weird about them liking us?

Erika shrugged. She said, Clearly they waited until the last minute to invite us.

I believed that Alexis had really been busy, that she'd meant to ask us—ask me—and gotten caught up, but if she had avoided asking me on purpose, it had been for a good reason. She had told me herself—it would be too tense, too much of a temptation. She'd shown me that that afternoon at her house. She would come up to me at the party and say, I'm sorry I didn't invite you, you're so cute, I didn't know if I'd be able to keep my hands off of you.

Erika said, Maybe it's just some swimming bonding thing. She took a photo from the top of the stack. There was no good system for ID-ing the people in them. If we didn't know who they were we had to match their faces to old yearbooks or walk around asking until we found someone who recognized them. Erika said, What's that girl's name again? I bet she'll be at that party. She said, I guess those girls are all right. She put the photo at the bottom of the pile. She said, But weird, right? Have you ever done a face mask?

I PASSED THE striver again. I almost passed Donna. After practice I saw Alexis talking with Coach about her turns and I stalled as long as I could before I got into the shower. I was in there with one other person and Alexis came in and got under the nozzle farthest from me. The other girl left. I said, Hey.

Alexis said, Hey. She was facing the wall and digging conditioner into her scalp so hard and fast I was afraid she'd gouge the skin. She said, Coach is making me stressed about my turns. He thinks I could shave off another second.

I didn't have any good advice about breaststroke turns. I said, I bet you'll do really great. You won last time. It was a stupid thing to say. I knew winning once had nothing to do with winning the next time. I said, I'm sorry.

Alexis said, What are you sorry for?

I said, Is it okay that I'm coming to the party?

She said, Of course, why wouldn't it be okay?

I wanted to say You know why. Not as an accusation. I wanted to ask why she hadn't called, or if I could have the number of her private line so I could call if I needed to.

Alexis turned off the shower and turned toward me. My body felt like an animal's. She said, The party's for the whole team. I'm glad you can come.

**WHEN I GOT** into the car my dad turned down the radio and asked, How's the training?

I said, It's okay. I said, You don't have to call it training.

My dad said, Sure. What do you call it?

I said, Calling it training makes it sound like I'm competitive. I wished I'd had something better to say to Alexis about her turns. I'd wanted to give Alexis something that could really help her. I felt like a poser, like the worst kind of striver. I said, It makes it sound like you want me to get into the Olympics or something.

My dad always drove slowly but now he slowed so much that the car behind us flashed its brights. My dad pulled over and the car sped around us. I said, Why are we stopping?

My dad said, Julie. You know your mother and I never want you to feel any pressure from us. Especially about swimming.

We were pulled over in front of the Taco Bell. I'd only eaten there once or twice but kids with cars, Alexis's friends, went to the drive-through during lunch and came back with crumpled burrito wrappers on their dashboards. A seven-layer burrito sounded amazing. It sounded so warm and complete. I almost asked my dad to pull into the driveway.

My dad said, You've got to tell me. Are we pushing you too hard?

I said, You're not pushing me at all. I didn't know what it would look like for them to be pushing me. They'd be asking when my meets were, offering to pay for extra lessons. They'd tell me what, that I couldn't have dinner until I won them a trophy? That I couldn't come home without a neckful of medals?

My dad said, Was it because of that magazine? All of Jordan's stuff?

I said, Was what because of it? I had never seen my dad like this before. His face looked like nothing was holding it together. It was worse than if he'd been crying. I wasn't sure if I knew enough about driving to drive us home, if it came to that.

My dad said, I told your mom that I thought you and Jordan might get closer when you got older. That's how it was with me and Uncle Dan.

My dad and his brother were best friends or like their version of best friends. I said, What did Mom say?

My dad laughed. Now he was crying a little, some wetness he wiped away. He said, She accused me of training you to be a spy.

I didn't really get it but I laughed with him.

ON THE FRIDAY of the meet Coach stood by the bus with his clipboard. The hood of my hoodie was up. I had on my parka and my gloves. If Coach stuck me in a relay I would quit right there. I would turn around and get off the bus. Coach looked at his clipboard, crossed something out, looked at me. He said, What do you say, Julie? You ready to give the 500 a go?

I said, Okay.


THE REFEREE BLEW his whistle to start the meet. It was a different referee from the last meet.

The Franklin swimmers wore black and gold.

Erika asked me if I was nervous. I said, A little.

I thought Alexis might look to me for luck before her races.

The bleachers cut into my thighs. Erika said I didn't need to be nervous, that I was going to kick ass.

The bleachers blew up in a cheer.

My legs fell asleep.

My legs bit and buzzed. I didn't have legs.

I couldn't swim without legs. I could, but I wouldn't— too much dead weight. I imagined Coach scooping me up and dropping me in.

Feet stamped metal and the bleachers shook.

The starting gun went and went.

I was tired. I leaned my head back against nothing.

Alexis stepped up on the block for the 100 Breast. If she looked at me, she might not acknowledge that she was looking at me, but I'd know it and she'd know it.

Alexis sliced the water. Her shoulders and head ducked and rose. I arrowed her luck. I pulled for easy turns. Her hips moved and I moved.

I said, I'm not really nervous.

Someone started We Are the Champions. Erika pulled my arm to get up and clap.

At the start of the 100 Butterfly, two races before mine, I stood up and stamped out the buzz in my legs. I went to the side of the bleachers to stretch. I held on to the pole of the bleachers with my right hand and bent my left leg behind me.

Alexis said, Hey Julie.

My hamstrings were tight. I switched legs. It was as if I hadn't swum in weeks.

She said, That's so great that you're swimming the 500. Are you nervous? She must have been used to winning by now but she still had the glow.

I said, A little.

She said, You're cute.

I said, What? I was surprised she'd said it right there, with everyone in possible earshot.

She said, I said that's really cute, that you're nervous. She said, Do you still want me to count laps for you?

I'd had a dream version of this day and in it I got to swim the 500 Free and Alexis, who was the reason I was swimming it, who'd been the first one to see that it might do something for me to swim it, was at the other end of the lane dipping numbers in the water to keep track of my laps. My edges burned. I said, I asked Erika.

She said, Oh. Okay.

I said, I didn't know if you'd remember. Now I couldn't remember if she'd actually offered or if it had only been part of the dream version. I said, I'm really sorry.

She said, No worries.

I said, I can tell Erika I changed my mind.

She said, No, your friend should do it. She said, Good luck, Julie, and put a smile on her face. It was the smile that cut a curved shape out of me and let the air rush through.

Because it was a home meet, I got to swim in my lane—my Lane Six, still, for now. Coach came over and put his hand on my shoulder. He said, Take it slow and steady. Just think of it as five 100s. He jostled my shoulder a little. He said, But no stopping, right? He tried to make it sound like a joke.

I curled my toes over the end of the starting block. At the other end of the lane, Erika waved and whistled and shook the counting board and looked very far away. The gun went and I went.

ERIKA WAS THERE at the finish to pull me out by my rubbery arms. She said, You did so great!

My breaths swayed my whole body. Nobody was left in the pool. The guys' 500 swimmers were already climbing on the blocks. I said, I didn't do great.

Erika put her arm around me. She said, Were you trying to win the gold?

I said, No.

Erika said, Right. I'm super proud of you. It felt like something a mom would say, but I was too exhausted to argue.

The gun went and the guys took off. Coach was in coach mode, yelling Pull!, slamming his hands together. I walked past expecting him not to notice me but he grabbed my elbow and pulled me back. He said, Julie. Nice job out there.

I said, Thanks. I said, I got pretty tired near the end.

He said, Comes with the territory. I followed his gaze out to the pool, where lanes of guy swimmers kept their pace up and tumbled from length seven to eight, from eight to nine. It was nothing tangible, nothing I could notice that made them move like that.

Erika came running over from the scorekeepers' table. She said, Jules, you got fifth place!

I said, No I didn't. I'd definitely been the last one in the pool. Unless I'd been so bleary that I'd missed another straggler? The last laps had felt uphill, but not impossible.

Erika explained that one of the Franklin swimmers had gotten disqualified for missing the wall on a flip turn.

I said, So it doesn't count.

Erika said, It does! You still get a point for fifth place.

I turned to ask Coach, but he was crouched toward the pool, red-faced and lunging, pulling for a swimmer who was going to win.

I said, I don't care about one point.

MELANIE LIVED IN a huge house so far out on Route 43 it might have been Lake Oswego. Erika and I got dropped off with our pillows and sleeping bags. We rang the bell and waited what felt like too long. There was obviously a party already going inside, loud music and lights on in all the downstairs windows. Erika tried the door and the latch was unlocked. I said, We should wait. Erika pushed the door open. We went in and stood in a big foyer with a chandelier. Alexis came in from a doorway without a door. She had a drink in her hand. She said, You made it! and stood there, and then came over and hugged Erika and hugged me. It was an idea of a hug, glancing, us all in the foyer, maybe because she also had to hug Erika, and we were still standing there holding all our things.

The house was huge and new. The carpet smelled new and in the huge living room were a big-screen TV and a very clean fireplace and other girls, mostly but not entirely swimmers. Melanie came in and hugged us and asked, Sea Breeze or screwdriver? The other girls were lying on couches or on the carpet, and they wore sweats and had their hair knotted up in buns and their faces full of makeup. Erika and I stood in the middle of the room in our jeans and no makeup. Erika might have been wearing lip gloss. Melanie brought us drinks in real glasses. She said, to the room, These girls are sopho-mores. They're swim team, and Yearbook. She said, And if you remember, Jordan Winter, the best swimmer in the history of Jackson? And super hot? She said, That's Julie's brother.

We threw our stuff in the pile in the corner. Grease was playing with the sound low. When a song came on, whoever had the remote would crank the volume. We had to watch the scene where Sandy and Danny rediscover each other at the pep rally three times. It was so embarrassing to watch Sandy's confused face while Danny played it cool and pretended he didn't know her. The girls on the carpet thought it was hilarious. I drank my drink. It must have been a Sea Breeze. I had Erika's bare foot and a bottle of nail polish in my lap. Alexis must have been in the kitchen, helping Melanie with snacks.

A girl, an okay butterflier, dove across a sleeping bag toward me. She said, So Julie? What is your brother doing now? She offered me a Werther's. She said, I forget, was he in the Olympics?

I took the Werther's. They were my favorite—warm and sweet and salty. I didn't care about this girl. I said, He almost made Seoul. He missed qualifying by a few seconds.

The girl said, That must have been so hard. She said, What do you do after something like that?

A girl I didn't know said, What a good question.

I had Erika's foot in my lap and I kept painting her big toe a dark plum. It was an ugly color. When I finished I'd find the polish remover and swab it off and start over. I didn't care that Erika could hear me. I said, He does something with computers. I said, He's married. He lives in Arizona, of all places. I painted Erika's toe so evenly and precisely I should have been a pedicurist.

I'd vaguely had to pee since we'd arrived, but I knew there would be only so many times I could escape to the toilet. I let Erika put nail polish on me—the palest, clearest pink—and I let my nails dry, and then I went wandering to find the bathroom. I peed and stood there for a while. I felt towels and sniffed shampoo. It was huge for a bathroom. I wished I could sleep in there.

Alexis was waiting outside the door when I got out. I apologized, embarrassed to have been in there so long, and she took my wrist and said, Come here. She led me down some stairs and through a mudroom to a back door and a slab of patio with deck chairs on it. It was cold out. She sat in one deck chair and I sat in another. She said, I'm sorry about not inviting you guys sooner. I was busy and I spaced it.

I said, It's okay. The dampness of the concrete seeped through my socks.

She said, You did a great job with the 500 today. I could tell from how she said it that she hadn't been watching. If I'd let her count laps for me, she would have been.

Alexis said, Listen Julie. I know I'm probably making a bigger deal of it, you're probably not even thinking about it, but just to be clear. I just wanted to tell you that I can't do that stuff we did anymore.

I said, Okay.

She said, I mean, I have a boyfriend.

I said, Okay.

She said, You probably will soon, too.

I didn't feel anything. I'd only been feeling one thing since the moment she had taken my wrist and said, Come here. I was waiting for her to kiss me. We weren't in her room or my room, or my house or her house. We were on a neutral slab of patio in the suburbs, a stage for anything.

She said, Sorry for making such a big deal about it. She said, I knew you'd understand.

In the living room, the girls were singing Hopelessly Devoted to You at the top of their lungs, swaying and pretending to drop perfumed paper into kiddie pools. Erika was singing, propped up in a nest of sleeping bags. Someone rewound the song to the beginning. Melanie pulled Alexis into a mock swoon against the bookshelf. It was as if Alexis had always been in there singing with them. In the lull at the end of the song, someone said, Did you hear something? No one had heard anything. Then someone else heard something, a pebble at a window, and it was as if it had been planned from the get-go, and maybe it had, as if it were a scene from a movie, at the big picture window that framed the living room was Grapestuff, and another boy, and another. There were masses of boys, clown cars of them, all the boys from swimming and beyond. And all the girls inside, with wet nails, shrieking.

Grease got turned off. Sleeping bags got pushed aside and the stereo got turned up, and the boys had beer and the girls refilled their cocktail cups. I filled mine half-way with vodka and added a splash of cranberry. A boy

I didn't know ducked into the kitchen and said, Slumber party! and knocked his cup against mine. I needed to find a couch with Erika on or near it. I needed a soft couch with enough cushions to bury myself in. Erika moved over on the couch to make room for me. She was laughing with two guys who looked like the opposite of PT—short and bulky, with hairy arms and crew cuts. Erika said, So what I want to know is, what do you do with the cup of spit when you're done with it? She said, They're wrestlers.

One of the guys said, Bottle it up and feed it to the losing team.

Erika said, Gross! She was loose and beaming.

The cool beige walls of the bathroom fortressed me. Against my cheek, my palm, they were what, marble? I pressed against the wall to soak in its smoothness. The face in the mirror didn't look like me. I opened the medicine cabinet and drawers and clicked around the orange bottles. What was the name of the pill I could take that could get me through the rest of the night, let me pass out with my sleeping bag in a little sister's room, in this bathroom? I didn't recognize the names on any of the labels.

I gulped my cocktail. I flushed the toilet. I ran the water hot on my hands. The last thing I wanted to do was to go back into the living room. It was the only place to go.

I heard them before I got there: shrieks and loud, exaggerated groans.

I heard a guy's voice—one of the wrestler's? Greg's?—saying, Oh yeah, do it again.

A girl's voice—Melanie's?—saying, Gross, I can't look!

It wasn't Melanie.

Because when I got back into the living room what I saw was a crowd gathered around in a circle, and at first I thought there was a fight going on. I thought maybe breakdancing, a performance. There were few enough people that I didn't have to push my way through. I just walked into the circle like anyone, just as one of the wrestlers said, One more time, and in the middle of the circle were Alexis and Melanie, looking coyly at each other and Alexis stepping forward and Melanie stepping forward and their mouths coming together and the two of them kissing, in huge, exaggerated swallows, in absolute blind passion. Someone said, Touch her tits, and Melanie put her hand underneath Alexis's shirt. I was drunk. I had a fever. I was so sure I was going to throw up that I told myself that was why I was running out of the room and back to the bathroom, and the door was locked, and I was sure that I had accidentally locked it behind me and there was no one in there and there was no way I'd ever get in there again.

I needed to find Erika because I needed to leave, before or because I was sick, and I couldn't stand the idea of seeing my parents but I could find Erika and we could call her mom, which would be all right. I hadn't seen her in the living room, thank god. I looked in the kitchen. I looked in every room of the house, my eyes hard set on finding her. The music was back up in the living room and the sideshow hoots were over. I was never going back in there. The only place left to look was outside. I went the way Alexis had led me, down the stairs and to the door of the mudroom and in there, leaning against the sliding-glass door to the patio, was Grapestuff, with his eyes closed, and Erika on her knees in front of him.

**THE OUTSIDE AIR** was cold. I didn't care. Thank god I'd left my shoes in the foyer. I'd grabbed the butterflier in the kitchen and told her to tell Erika that I'd gone home and was fine. The butterflier said, Which one was she? I told her to ask Erika to bring home my stuff.

Ben pulled up in his old tan car. He said, You were right about this being way the fuck out here.

I said, Thanks for coming. The car heater was on high, guitar music low from the speakers.

Ben said, No jacket? He said, I'm not going to ask if you're okay, because obviously you're not.

I said, I'm fine.

Ben said, Something with a boy?

I said, No.

Ben drove. He was driving back a different way than we'd come, up a wide road with a million old neon motel signs. The signs were bright flashing colors, improbable palm trees, broken bulbs. The signs went on for miles. Ben said, A girl?

The fabric of the car seat was the softest thing I'd ever felt. My face was all over it. I was snot and free feelings pouring all over the inside of Ben's car.

Ben's hand on my shoulder was warm, a true cup, a gauze. He said, Oh, little sister.

WHEN I WOKE up on the couch, Ben was still asleep. I wrote a note and took the key he'd said to take if I woke up before him. It was misty out. The cemetery went on for blocks. The tombstones were dark with rain or age. Nothing about walking in a cemetery felt inherently sad. No people buried in there wouldn't be dead by now no matter how young they'd died.

I felt blank. The only thought from last night that I let myself think about was Erika in the mudroom. I had hated seeing it, but I could think about Erika and what could have brought her there and worry, thoughtfully, about whether she was okay and whether, in leaving, I'd left her to something more terrible. I knew her mom had been set to pick us up at 9:00 AM, and the pay phone in front of the Plaid Pantry was free.

Erika said, My god, Julie, what happened?

I said, I started feeling really sick, and I just had to go. I'm sorry I couldn't tell you before I left.

Erika said, What kind of sick? From the vodka?

I said, Maybe.

Erika said, So you just called your dad to come get you?

I said, I didn't call my dad. The drinking and everything. I said, I called my friend Ben.

Erika said, Who's Ben?

I said, The older guy.

Erika said, No way! What about his girlfriend?

I almost said I'm his girlfriend. My heart pitched and caught. The sky was smooth and gray, the shell of an egg that couldn't hatch. I said, He has a boyfriend, actually.

Erika said, Oh wow, really?

I said, It's not a big deal.

Erika said, When did he tell you? Or did you just know?

I said, I kind of knew.

Erika said, I know what you mean. She said, That's too bad, though. A lot of gay guys are really cute. She sounded normal, like Erika, her voice a little hollow and tired.

I said, It was nice of him to come all the way out there to get me.

Erika said, Yeah, it was. Then we didn't say anything. I wasn't going to ask about Grapestuff in the mudroom. She could tell me if she wanted to. Erika said, You know, those girls and those guys are okay, but I don't think they're really our people.

I said, I guess.

Erika said, You know who is actually nice, though? Alexis. She was asking me where you were.

As I was trying to fall asleep on Ben's couch, I'd gotten racked with doubt about having left the party. Not because I was worried about Erika, though that should have been why, but because it had suddenly seemed possible that after the guys had left or the hoots died down, Alexis would find me again and tell me that she hadn't meant what she'd said on the patio, or, more likely, she wouldn't mention what she'd said on the patio but she would ignore it, taking me by the wrist to a guest bed, a sister's bedroom, and everything would be the way it had been.

I said, So nothing else exciting happened after I left?

Erika said, Is learning how to play beer pong exciting?

We said we'd talk again later in the day. I had only stood in the doorway of the mudroom for such a quick second, maybe it hadn't been Erika in there. She seemed completely fine.

Ben was flipping through records. He said, Are you the kind of person who likes to hear sad music when you're sad, or angry music?

I said, I listen to the same music all the time. I thought of the wince and the whine, the fervent longing in Country Feedback. I said, What do you mean by angry music?

Ben said, Let's go with loud guitars. I think that'll do you good. Unless you're hungover?

The beginning of the song Ben put on sounded like a chainsaw without a tree, and the chainsaw sound kept on in the background while the drums did a military march. The singer sounded pissed and languid, as if no one could make him feel worse or better. There was a line about someone being shot, and a line about all men being slime. That chainsaw growl was louder than my feelings but also a version of them, their loud unspooling. Ben said, People will tell you that old Sonic Youth is better, and I'm not going to argue, but that is a fucking good song.

I said, Will you tape it for me?

Ben got out a big metal bowl and started mixing batter. He said, Coffee or tea? and gave me a ceramic jar of tea bags to look through. He said, You know, I've been thinking about that bitch Alexis.

I said, She's not a bitch.

Ben said, I know, I'm sorry. She's not a bitch.

I hadn't told Ben about every single thing, but I had told him enough. I said, I didn't think she even liked Melanie that way.

Ben said, She probably doesn't. It's a thing, straight guys like to see two girls get it on.

I said, That's stupid.

Ben said, I know.

There was some small relief in knowing it had been a show. Or maybe that made it worse. I said, Do you think that's why Alexis did stuff with me, too?

Ben poured a pale circle of batter into the pan. He said, No, I think she really liked you. He edged the spatula around the circle and said, And who knows, maybe she likes Melanie or Melanie likes her too. Those girls have got issues.

That made me laugh. Only Ben would say they were the ones with the issues.

**ON THE BUS** ride home I put my head against the window. I hadn't slept enough. When I got home I'd get into bed and sleep as long as I wanted. I'd tell my parents we'd stayed up until dawn watching movies. They wouldn't care. I'd tell them I was exhausted from swimming the 500, and they wouldn't ask me how I'd done because they didn't want to put any pressure on me. They wouldn't ask me and so I wouldn't tell them how in the middle of the race, after Erika had dipped 11 and I knew I'd made it halfway through, I'd felt a sort of high. The water held me and I was sure I was schooling it, that Coach would see me and let me stay in Lane Six. If Alexis had seen me in that brief moment when I was on rails, I was on air, she would have decided to dump Greg and forget Melanie and choose me. Or she'd have kept whoever she wanted and kept choosing me, which was selfish, so what. She'd promise me I was her favorite when I told her everything I knew about my brother—how he was in Berlin for good, staying up all night, not swimming, killing us with his dying by not telling us.

It was raining, surprise, hard enough that I could see where the drops sunk holes in the river's skin. I wished I had my Walkman. I wished I had it and that Ben had already taped that Sonic Youth song for me so I could put it on loud and the clawed guitars could tear and balm me. The bus got to the west side and passed the River Market, where shoppers crowded under the stalls' awnings to stay dry. I would call Erika back later, after my nap. I might tell her Ben and my brother had fooled around in high school. She might ask me more about Ben's boyfriend. I'd tell her I hadn't met him yet, but that I'd heard he was really cute. I might tell her they'd met at a bar called the Anchor, just to see what she'd say.

## ACKNOWLEDGMENTS

Thank you to the Regional Arts and Culture Council, Virginia Center for the Creative Arts (VCCA), Vermont Studio Center, and RADAR Lab for providing me with space and time to write this book. Thank you to Masie Cochran for being dedicated to *Dryland* and for your amazing ability to know what's not enough and what's too much, and to the rest of the Tin House crew. Thank you to Mark Jaffe, for being my brother and always my friend. Thank you to the many writing teachers I have had over the years—particularly Noy Holland, who helped me see that language is everything, and Camille Roy, who split open my sense of what narrative could do. Thank you Lynne Tillman for caring about young writers. My writing community/support network is spread out like points of light on a map and I am so glad it includes Jason Daniel Schwartz, Andrea Lawlor, Sara Marcus, Amanda Davidson, Megan Milks, Leni Zumas, Susan Steinberg, Alicia Jo Rabins, Samiya Bashir, Pete Rock, Susan Carlton, Donal Mosher, Mike Palmieri,

Lucy Corin, Michelle Tea, and Lidia Yuknavitch, whose advice and feedback at various points in the process were invaluable. For being my number-one reader back since our days holding writing group at The Gatekeeper, thank you Jess Arndt, brilliant writer, reader, and friend. Thank you to Noah Hazel in ways I don't know yet. And infinitely huge thank you to Nadia Cannon, for supporting me in every way possible through the writing of this book, and always making me feel capable and loved.